Marcus Samuel Cam Rickards

Lyrics and Elegiacs

Marcus Samuel Cam Rickards

Lyrics and Elegiacs

ISBN/EAN: 9783744787468

Printed in Europe, USA, Canada, Australia, Japan

Cover: Foto ©Andreas Hilbeck / pixelio.de

More available books at **www.hansebooks.com**

LYRICS AND ELEGIACS.

LYRICS AND ELEGIACS

BY

MARCUS S. C. RICKARDS

AUTHOR OF " CREATION'S HOPE," "SONGS OF UNIVERSAL LIFE,"

ETC.

LONDON

GEORGE BELL & SONS, YORK ST., COVENT GARDEN

AND NEW YORK

1893

CHISWICK PRESS :—C. WHITTINGHAM AND CO., TOOKS COURT, CHANCERY LANE.

CONTENTS.

ERRATA.

Page 28, line 4, *for* " Of an unearthly Clime " *read* " That bars her haunt Divine."

Page 43, line 13, *for* " hurled " *read* " whirled."

Page 82, line 10, *for* " thought " *read* " talk."

Page 99, line 21, *for* " fields " *read* " plains."

Page 107, line 1, *for* " ay " *read* " for."

Page 109, line 21, *for* " nerve and bone " *read* " nerves and bones."

Page 117, line 6, *for* " downcast " *read* " downbent."

Page 121, between lines 19 and 20, *read* " While loftier instincts claim their due."

Page 125, line 7, *for* " germinate " *read* " vegetate."

A

LYRICS AND ELEGIACS.

PRELUDE.

MY song is born of rivalry. Cross Time,
So leaden winged when he should speed apace—
So swift when, breathing some enchanted clime,
Or spellbound by the magic of some face,
We fain would fetter him—cross Time has left
One golden scene behind for near a year,
One scene that would not linger, yet no theft
From Memory's store shall make it disappear :
A pleasant scene it was, a fairy spot,
A happy hour when I was one of three.
Tho' "two be company while three are not "
That homely saw was falsified, for we
Held sweet communion mid delightful strife.
The Muses we discussed ; each bowed to one,
And found therein the solace of a life,
So for this pleaded as a central sun
Round which the rest revolved. One lively friend
Claimed excellence for Painting, that appealed
To sight, the queen of senses. Artists blend,
She urged, Earth's beauty with the grace concealed
Within, and fusing them in lovely form
Fix fleeting charms that many scarce behold—

B

Interpret Nature, and the multiform
Complexities of human life unfold—
Obliquely teach, and silently impress,
And by the witchery of Colour's spell
Wake up the taste, the truth, the tenderness
That sleep within us all.　She pleaded well,
So well that seemingly she fanned the flame
That fired the friend beside her (both were fair)
Who worshipped Music and had won a name.
In tremulous tones she asked what could compare
With harmony, that served a subtle sense
More delicate than vision, more refined?
What rouse more surely love, awe, reverence?
What stronger lever to uplift the mind?
What better balsam for an aching core?
What truer tonic?　'Tis a certain key
Whereby the spirit's many-chambered store
May be unlocked, and prisoned wealth set free:
How feeling, fancy, memory, even will
Unbar their bolts to married tune and time!
How a rapt audience yields responsive thrill
To its enchanter! and how hearts that chime
With his, divine the meaning of each mood!
And then both turned to me who sang the praise
Of Poetry.　My Muse all worthy stood
Small chance when I confronted their quick gaze
And smart replies: and yet I proved her strong,
Strongest, methinks, in this, that human thought,
And feeling, too, perchance, sustain least wrong
Thro' her exacter voice obscuring naught.
The Painter in his silence scarce atones
By fine suggestion for his impotence
To limn the full effect of Nature's tones,

PRELUDE.

That charm and teach thro' vocal eloquence:
While the Musician, pouring out his heart,
What can he language to a kindred soul
But vague idea and feeling? what impart
Save as an outlined fructifying whole?
At utmost he recounts a thrilling tale
That all enjoy but none quite comprehend;
Whose forms and scenes and acts in true detail
Live not in those who fondest audience lend.
The Poet only in his verbal might
Transmits exactly, and completely tells:
Let him bewitch the reader's inward sight
By deft word-colouring, and he excels
The Painter-champion—let his verse have grace
Of rhythm, cadence, and fine subtle shades
Of harmony, and the Musician's place
Is scarce as high.   But no! the rival maids
Linked hands in laughing league to overthrow
My lofty claim—and hence these various rhymes;
A poor attempt to make the scorners know
That Poetry, if rich in hues and chimes
Of verbiage, by virtue of her power
Unique of full transmission, wins the palm.
We pledged each other that the trysting bower,
Which shed around us then such fragrant balm,
Should circle us anew a twelvemonth hence,
When I should read my poems: and perchance
This failure will at least yield evidence
Of what success might prove; and so the lance,
Unsheathed in loyal battle for my Muse,
Tho' splintered may win honour for her name.
Meanwhile, methinks, I hardly need excuse
This humble volume tho' it earn no fame :

The Painter vaunts the labours of a year
And welcomes critics to his studio;
Musicians covet that the world should hear
Their tuneful work, and praise or blame bestow.
Deem this my " private view," my " open night,"
Or what you will, but hold it true no less,
That I have failed, tho' even I delight,
Save where I lift, and purify, and bless!

AN ARTIST'S APOSTROPHE.

TOO often they linger apart,
  Gloomy Toil and bright Beauty;
But lo! forged in fire of my heart
  See the clasp of hard Duty;
Pure gold, like the midsummer sun,
  Full rounded, fine fashioned,
The circlet that links two in one
  By a life-vow impassioned.

Dull Toil! Nature marks thee as groom,
  For thy force, thews, and muscle;
They fit thee to win ample room
  'Mid life's pressure and bustle:
Tho' Sin was thy sire, in the sweat
  Of thy brow lurks a blessing;
Thy dews health and glory beget,
  Tho' born of transgressing.

Fair Beauty! as bride must thou shine;
   Eternity's splendour
Has robed thee in vesture divine,
   Of hues soft and tender;
Appear, radiant daughter of Truth!
   From thy Mansion above him;
Upraise him from Time's gloom and ruth,
   Serve, honour, and love him!

He, taken for better or worse,
   With strength shall endow her;
While she lifts the lingering curse
   That o'er him may lower.
Sweet pair! Heaven formed you to mate;
   To-day shall ye marry;
This ring the true token that Fate
   Constrains you to tarry,

To tarry, for aye in my heart
   With Bliss for your neighbour;
If Toil support Beauty in Art
   And Beauty crown Labour,
Then, born of the twain, a bright throng
   Of Graces shall cherish
All Right in my work, and its Wrong
   Shall faint, fade, and perish.

ODE TO A REDBREAST.

THE darling thou of many a heart,
Who warblest ere the year depart
   One last clear note of praise,
Sweet echo of the silenced song
Of summer minstrels, lingering long
To wean dark Nature from the wrong
   Of these sad autumn days!

O joy, that blithe notes from above
Break Death's monotony with Love,
   Calm Faith and cloudless Hope!
Beneath, dank fallen leaves decay,
Around, is settled sunless grey,
When lo! thy music from yon spray,
   "Look up, nor weakly mope!"

Responsive notes from some nigh bough
Repeat the strain, and disallow
   Gloom's menace of return;
Divine duet—appeal, reply!
Adieu despondency and sigh!
With ravished ear, and wistful eye,
   I listen, look, and learn.

Thou angel link 'tween heaven and earth!
Did Seraphs supervise thy birth,
   And lend thee guise and tune?

Stamp on thy gorget a true sign
That pent within is fire divine,
As flaming at the year's decline
  As mid sweet golden June?

Mere Nature would inspire no strain,
But cloud thy peace with yearnings vain,
  Dark fears, and wild regrets.
Spring's vanished joy is scarce forgot.
The gentle mate, the trysting grot,
The ivied bank, the mossy spot
  Begemmed with violets.

And instinct draws no kindly veil
O'er nearing frost, and snow, and hail,
  Spare shelter, scanty food.
Nay that bright eye, that flashing gleam,
Hint that a Genius sits supreme,
To gild near darkness with the dream
  Of sunny, distant good.

The carol with thy cheery friend
Is Hope's forecast of winter's end,
  Faith's interim repose:
'Tis that I doubt not—and this more
Perchance—the interflow of lore
About some strange unearthly shore
  Your after lot—who knows?

At least your music wafts this truth,
" Forget past joyaunce, present ruth,
  Near griefs, impending ill, *ruee,*

ODE TO A REDBREAST.

In commune with true hearts of light
And bliss, yet stored for mortal sight,
And what fair vision of Delight
   Thy glancing Heaven may show!"

A SONG FOR THE WEARY.

SEEMS it so sad and strange
That in the world's wide range
Hearts vexed by toil and change
   Find not repose?
Man, thou art but a guest!
Earth spreads for thee her best;
Her rarest to thy quest
   She will disclose:

Yet has she never heard,
Never, of one soft word;
No faery bee or bird
   Sets it to song:
Rest is the word, and lo!
To some sweet Long-ago,
All of it thou dost know
   Can but belong.

Could fierce winds teach it thee?
Could the inconstant sea?
Could soft play o'er the lea
   Of glancing beam?

ON A PACKET OF OLD LETTERS.

Moon and stars know it not :
Even men have forgot
The dear lore of past lot,
    In life's sad dream.

But that kind Seraphs flit
Round thee to whisper it,
Would not false Sense outwit
    Memory's truth ?
But for the spirit's fire,
But for the heart's desire,
But that Earth's pleasures tire
    Even fresh youth,

Seek it here, if thou must,
'Mid strife, and loss, and rust,
To find in mortal dust
    Earth's only rest !
Seek it in Bliss of old,
Glory to be retold ;
And find a God will fold
    Thee to His breast !

ON A PACKET OF OLD LETTERS.

THE choicest blooms that ever blent,
In one sweet posy have decayed;
And then,—adieu to charm and scent !
    Naught lingers when they fade :

But lo! to these a perfume clings,
These memories of vanished things,
These spent effusions—each a flower
Of love that blossomed for its hour.

I lit upon them laid aside
Mementoes of a happier day,
When Life was Beauty, Hope, and Pride,
    And Time, one lingering May :
Sole relics of a kindred host,
Each seems like a returning ghost
Of glory in the tender Past ;
Or some dead joy, embalmed to last :

For as I read, a shadowy crowd
Of fresh young faces smile and glow—
Girls soft and fair, boys brave and proud,
    My mates of long ago.
What pledges passed, what vows and sighs !
See here their tokens ! my replies—
Ah ! where are they, now Death has strewn
Their treasure, and spared mine alone ?

Too strange, too sad that these outlive
The heads that thought, the hands that penned !
The writings should be fugitive
    The writers know no end !
So must it be ; the love that found
An outlet thus can brook no bound :
'Tis somewhere, and shall volume gain,
From barriers that now restrain !

Dear hearts ! our commune is not spent :
Methinks your missives reach me still,
In hopes by happy angels sent,
  Which Love shall yet fulfil ;
And one bright Morning, as of old
Our voices chime, Where all is told,
Where spirits throb in cloudless truth,
Unshadowed joy, immortal youth !

THE COMMON LOT.

CALL it not vain, this life
Teeming with care, and strife,
    Change, decay, pain,
Sorrow spent, anguish kept,
Hope dispelled, tears unwept :
Ay, tho' the worst still slept,
    Call it not vain !

Not while the seasons change,
Not till winds cease their range,
    Till tides delay,
Till beasts, and birds of earth,
Sport in unshadowed mirth,
Till sad Night brings to birth
    No chequered Day.

Nature of peace knows naught ;
All is thro' tumult brought

Safe to its prime :
Reft of gloom, gale and snow
Adieu sweet meadow show !
Cowslips and violets blow
    Mid tearful clime.

But for tempestuous seas
Calm barques might sleep at ease,
    Havenward bound.
Genius, when storms are rife,
Blooms ; and a nation's strife
Shapes the commanding life
    All rally round.

Art's triumph ponder too,
Ye that crave ease, yet woo
    Fame for her best !
Yon master-piece was born
Of sweet fond faith outworn—
Nursed in a heart forlorn—
    Fed on unrest.

Beauty's supremest grace
Lurks in a chastened face ;
    Joy quenching ruth.
Love, that can scorn decay,
Knows more of cloud than ray—
Thro' hindrance fights its way,
    Buying its truth.

Angels and Saints at rest !
Ye who decipher best
    Life's puzzling tale ;

Lend us, faint wrestlers here,
Vision full keen to peer,
Courage to persevere,
  Strength to prevail!

LIMITATIONS.

THOU cravest sympathy? Yet never think
  It wafts us past the brink
  Of the dark gulf that parts
The mysteries of even wedded hearts :
Love's utter spell no potency imparts
  That solemn deep to bridge,
And can but guide the spirit to its border ridge.

And there they peer at vision's utmost bourn,
  Two baffled souls forlorn,
  Each on opposing height,
No Pisgah with the Promised Land in sight,
But shrouded in the mists of hopeless Night,
  Till sadly they retreat
Back to the sunny realm where thoughts and feelings
    meet.

For there at least awaits them the sweet boon
  Of shadowless commune :
  There each can think and say,
And both shall mingle in divinest play,
For naught is dim, since all is golden Day.

Fair hope ! yet is it so ?
We who have lingered longest sadly murmur " No."

Perchance 'mid lonely acres may be found
    One rood of common ground,
    One happy trysting place
Where hot emotions rushing in embrace
To fondly mingle for a little space :
    And Earth has naught of bliss
Compared with what is born of interflow like this.

But back too soon upon the lonely plain
    We seek to blend, in vain ;
    And things that flame one breast
Chill like spent embers fallen from the rest :
Few glowing thoughts and fancies when confessed
    Meet with responsive fire ;
So private is the vision, the creation, the desire !

So secret too the joy, the grief, the hope,
    That Truth scarce finds due scope
    For play ! We talk and smile
Yet feel we skate on thinnest ice the while :
Anon the plunge—and rescued hearts beguile
    The hour that promised fair
For weighty fond converse, with trifles light as air.

We reason oft, we wage a war of words,
    That shames the strife of birds
    Who on sad autumn eves
Hold shrill discussion 'mid the fading leaves ;
But do we argue for what each believes ?

Nay ; rampant 'mid the tide
Of repartee are vanity, self-love and pride.

And there are things whereof the shy heart dreams,
   Unutterable themes,
   Shunned skilfully by each
Amid the eddying babble of that stream of speech,
Like half-hid boulders in a brooklet's reach
   Round, which the waters swirl
A moment, to flow blithely on in silvery purl.

And will it ever be, my wistful Friend,
   That ampler sense shall lend
   Our spirits insight true
To pierce each other's being thro' and thro'?
I doubt not then that to my ravished view
   Undreamt of wealth will show
How much I dwarfed and wronged thy nature here
      below !

A REVERIE ON HATHERLEY
CHURCHYARD.

NAY, mock me not with shifting human smiles,
Or Nature's light and shade in glistening play !
Oft, fickle Beauty ! have I marked thy wiles,
Too oft, the winning glance, the sunny ray
Die in the birth of a dark frown.   That spell
Has lost its witchery for one who knows it well.

Change is thy potent charm; but ah! poor hearts,
Dupes of its ruin, we ask more than this—
Somewhat to hint, when chequered glow departs,
That in the background lurks unchanging bliss:
Tho' none could face thy glory here and live,
This may we see, and this I know that thou canst give:

I know it, for I oft the power have felt,
When Music, thy sweet minister, would lure,
Of one note dominant: where all had spelt
Confusion else, that note throughout secure
Sustained the harmony, and lent thee wings
To flit and flash and dazzle with unearthly things.

Oft when I dream has one pure golden thought,
Fixed mid wild riot, seemed to gild the whole:
Oft Morn before my waking sight has brought
The dear home faces, each informed with soul
Of tested love, that leaves expression free
To pout in transient gloom or sparkle with bright glee.

Yea, well I know it, and then best of all
When thou by means of one sweet sylvan scene
Hast held my spirit in delicious thrall.
If ever mortal eyes have pierced thy screen
To vision thee uncurtained, it was there,
For Earth scarce holds a picture more divinely fair.

Ay, fair as changeful; changeful as first Love,
That flushes, flames and glows, to faint and die:
Frail as new Grief, that like the storm above,
Sinks from wild hurricane to tender sigh:

Moody as Fortune, that in one brief year
Oft varies poverty with wealth, and smile with tear.

So alternates that scene—a holy Rood
Flanked by far hills beyond a swelling plain,
With trees and saplings studded, and dense wood,
Mid many a smiling field, and witching lane,
In guise attuned to each celestial boon,
Sunbeam, cloud, tempest, evening breeze, and silvery
    moon.

And yet for all its magic impotent
To win the wistful spirit, save that here
With show of change, eternal Rest is blent,
Born of the quiet Church that year by year
Stands central and unvaried to proclaim
That mid Earth's shifting scenes calm Heaven is the
    same.

And circling evergreens repeat the Tale,
Like bodied echoes that have sunk to Earth,
And risen in fixed forms that never fail ;
Or spirits lingering near to temper mirth,
Vested in dark unfading guise, the more
To fetter fickle Fancy to the changeless Shore.

Mid tender April verdure, snow of May,
June green, September gold, October fire,
The massive Tower retains its hoary grey,
In grandeur that seems scarcely to require
Support from yellow elm and burnished beech,
And all the Seasons' splendour, far as eye can reach,

Save as a Monarch needs his spangled dress,
A Judge his ermined scarlet, or a Priest
His snowy robe, to silence and impress;
Save as a high-born Dame resolves to feast
With deep design a suitor's ravished gaze
On rich apparel, varying with various days.

Too feeble similes! for what high King,
What Judge severe, what Priest with blessing fraught,
What Charmer of rapt hearts could ever bring
Such might, truth, comfort, love, as that has brought
Whereto yon Temple witnesses—which sounds
For many an hour Divine within its sacred bounds.

Ah! measured thus, no emblem seems too high:
The solemn Church, so calm amid decay,
So stern mid waxing glory, how shall I
Belaud such simple grandeur? Shall I say
Eternal Fact, mid fancies of vain time?
Mid fiction light and airy, Poetry sublime?

Celestial Truth, mid fluctuating forms
Born of Earth's falsity and mortal need?
The Christian Faith outweathering the storms
That wreck its fragile garniture? The Creed
Cinctured by an ephemeral pageantry
Outworn and doomed, but which Itself can never die?

The " Kingdom not of this world " vainly graced
With earthly pomp, and backed by temporal power
Whose grandeur falls like trembling leaves when faced.
By Autumn's panoply—frost, wind and shower?

And any loftier name high Fancy gives,
That surely claims which, when all else has faded, lives.

And as that Temple charms the wandering eye,
Unquiet souls are wooed by the sweet Sum
Of what it shadows, what its Rites supply,
The Grace, the Mercy, shed on all who come,
The Hope whose firm support heart-tendrils grasp,
As ivy creepers cling to the old Tower they clasp.

And Fancy bids me note that nigh this Fane
Are human growths, like the fair clustering trees,
That bloom and wither here —who know life's pain,
And joy; some toilers, some who live in ease,
None franchised of the laws of vital change,
Not rooted in one spot but free to move and range.

Nor plant-like, with contemporaneous dower
Of sun or shade, but each in solitude
Of special lot; o'er this dark storm-clouds lower;
O'er that the azure smiles; and none intrude,
On others' destiny: each mortal life
Takes shape and colour from its girdling calm and
　　　strife.

I, but a guest here, scarce could know it true,
But that one village miniatures the world;
Nay, all the human story glimmers through
One rustic life.　As ocean gems empearled
Within their shells, all spirits live the same
In mortal casement, with like purpose, hope and aim:

Yet as a fading landscape, how diverse
Their waning history, their seeming end !
All, green in youth, unmarred by mortal curse ;
In age, what sombre tints and bright hues blend!
What shades, from gold to grey, from flame to rust,
Keep lingering state till each yields to the wintry gust !

Strange human tale ! Would that I read it clear !
This only know I—Autumn's varied scene,
Sad tho' it be, is loveliest of the year.
Perchance this visioned from the Clime serene,
Smiles tenderly—this web all weave ; for none
Evades the Passion-loom where Character is spun,

Whence issue moral threads that intertwine
To make the texture, and impart the tone,
Beneath the impress of a Power Divine
That harmonizes all, to whom is known
All potency for good or bad ; and who
By Life's experience evolves the false, the true.

Lo! imaged clearly here, see tranquil Bliss
Calm as a dreamy Elm ; unselfish Grace
That like an Aspen quivering to the kiss
Of plaintive zephyrs suns a radiant face
Athrill with sympathy ; and pleased Desire,
With music like a swaying Birch, as from a wind-
        swept lyre.

Here fragrant Kindness like a perfumed Lime
Charms to herself a murmuring, grateful throng :
While vain Remorse, as if bemoaning crime,
Droops like a weeping Willow : and rude Wrong

Keen and red-fruited like a Holly, sheds
A deepening shadow as his prickly empire spreads;

And quaking Fear here blanches to each breath
Like silvery Sallows; and the pensive Pine
Rapt Melancholy broods like dusky Death,
Impervious to each sunbeam that would shine
And gender comfort; while in lonely gloom,
Bereavement like a shadowy Cedar haunts her tomb;

Here empty Passion bends to Destiny,
As blighted Lilacs to the chilly blast;
And hopeless Love aspires to the far sky,
Like a sad Cypress, lofty tho' downcast;
And wild Despair bewails, with arms up-tossed,
Like leafless Ash boughs, joys, once fresh, for ever lost.

Here see dark Hate, that, like a baneful Yew,
Sheds poison round: and chastened Grief now healed,
Which, youthful still, is scarred and silvered too
Like a pale Plane, whose bark is semi-peeled;
And Fortitude, that as a hardy Oak
Outlives fierce storms, nor totters till the woodman's
          stroke;

And more—nay all—all passions, and each state,
Whatever sways humanity, see here!
For most possess each mortal soon or late.
And some they soften, some, alas! they sear,
Perchance but for a while, since radiant Hope
Whispers that Righteous Love would limit else their
          scope.

I never watch the flashing sunbeams paint
A lovely Rainbow on the tearful gloom
Behind this graveyard, but I hold my plaint
For outcast souls, and trust that utter doom
Has shadowed none—that Heaven in the far
Dim Future may for each the shining Gates unbar.

This Skyward Tower bears witness to the Might
That now welds all in a consummate whole—
The glorious Energy that, as the Light
Wherein all live and grow, plays round each soul ;
At *this* but glancing, leaving *that* in shade,
Whose glow encircles all that flourish, all that fade.

Beauty ! to Thee I sing ! that Light art Thou :
'Tis but Thy phantom that suffuses Space,
And chequers Earth, save when I pierce as now,
Helped by some tranquil type, thro' Nature's grace
To Thee, its high Dispenser, and behold
In human Character thy traces manifold.

And when it saddens me that, spite of Thee
Naught lovely lingers long—so much is vile,
So little fair in Man, I seem to see
A final burst of Glory, quenching guile,
One last blaze o'er mortality down-trod,
For Thou art Righteousness, and Love, and Christ,
        and God !

PROGRESS.

MID faery voices, none
Haunts my repose like one,
Faintly, Delight begun,
    Clear at its best.
Calm as a spirit tone
From the Eternal Throne,
Wafted to me alone,
    " On ! from thy rest."

When I expect it least—
When Beauty spreads her feast,
Flaming West, flushing East
    Gilding Noon's blue :
When Art has lured my soul
By hope of Fame's bright scroll ;
When Toil has bid some goal
    Flash on my view :

When Truth, with beckoning hand,
Charms from soft level land,
And climbing up, I stand
    On the pure Mount :
When Love furls golden wings
Nigh some sweet bower, and sings
Of the bright, dreamy things
    No heart can count :

When, led by Duty's gleam
'Mid gloom and thorns, I seem

Graced by her crown supreme
All to have won ;
When, as from stainless skies,
Virtue bends favouring eyes,
Holding a victor's prize
For race well run,

" On ! " sings the seraph voice ;
" Ease is not Wisdom's choice ;
None who recline rejoice,
None, low or high :
On, to the best of earth !
On, raised in loftier Birth,
On, to undreamt of worth,
On, on for aye ! "

VANISHED !

I SAW her first as when one sees
Some wingèd guest that the night breeze
Has sped from a far clime :
So suddenly she met my eyes ;
Her dreamy look, her lovely guise,
Like one whose commune with the skies
Out-distanced Space and Time.

Her voice was as the warbling heard
At sunrise, from a tuneful bird,
That rapt hearts linger nigh :

Her accents charmed me, and I stayed
Spellbound at every tone that strayed
From lips predestined to persuade
    By whisper, song, or sigh.

Her ways were as the minstrel's pose
That flits o'er woodbine and wild rose,
    And hovers round to bless ;
To steep the joyless heart in mirth ;
To lift the sordid soul from earth
And bid it covet loftier worth,
    Ethereal loveliness.

My wintry heart at once knew Spring ;
And Summer perfume seemed to cling
    Around her smile and breath :
But while her grace my vision flamed,
She vanished ; for one surely aimed—
A fowler lurking near—and claimed
    The due of lordly Death.

A DREAM OF PERFECTION.

I FOUND it in a vision fair—
All I had ever longed to find—
A face illumed by beauty rare
    That ravished heart and mind,
With smile like sunlit waves, and eyes,
Whose blue disdained the sapphire skies—

A form superb whose lines and hue
No classic pencil ever drew.

And all, tho' wondrous bright, excelled
In glory by the quickening soul
That shone thro' the sweet face and held
    The figure in control.
I felt that Virtue here displayed
What threw Mortality in shade—
Love, Truth and Purity, whose birth
Owed naught of parentage to Earth.

And yet, so wayward is a dream,
She looked like no unearthly guest,
But just a woman, and supreme,
    As of her sex the best ;
Before me flashed the archetype
Of my imaginings, the ripe
Perfection, that in sanguine hour
I deemed might haunt a mortal bower.

Ah me ! that we should be the sport
Of wild expectancy—that none
Of all with whom we here consort
    May prove the hoped-for one.
We mingle, for each soul to paint
Her high ideal, soon to faint
As rude experience re-shows
The shadow cast by all that glows.

Our spirits weave a web of light
Round one whose casual look has power

To overcloud the image bright
    Which fails us from that hour.
Or we who in each other's eyes
Read love and truth, with sad surprise,
Find coolness, guile, a shattered spell,
A sunny heaven changed to hell.

And so before such faultless grace
Of form and spirit low I bent;
And on me lingers still the trace
    Of lofty passion spent.
For who shall blame my wild regret,
When half awake, with eyelids wet
I knew my radiant guest had flown,
And I, fond dreamer, was alone?

Alone—and shall I never meet
The one for whom my spirit sighs?
Must Time and Sense for ever cheat
    And visions tantalize?
Nay—for as water to its source
Will rise—as naught owns empty force,
Whate'er the shaping soul conceives
That fully, fondly, she receives.

We long, long hopelessly, we think,
For Truth in human guise, and lo!
'Twas mine, when hovering on the brink
    Of Earth's dark portico.
Yet the fair visitant was more
Than Fancy fashions from her store.
Sleep! was all vain, all fugitive,
When thou to Adam Eve couldst give?

Ah! what if in pre-natal state
I loved some spirit, only mine,
When dreams unlock the golden gate
    Of an unearthly Clime?
Or maybe happy Heaven cast
The shade before of what at last
I shall behold, admire, embrace
A perfect soul, and form, and face.

ODE TO THE EARLIEST SNOWDROP.

CHASTE flower, I fear to do thee wrong!
The first-born of a stainless throng
Might claim as delicate a song
    As poet ever wrought.
I covet no diviner theme;
To look upon thee is to dream
Of Joy and Loveliness supreme
    Above terrestrial thought.

Pure child of Winter's ripe old age
By fresh young Spring! thy parentage
Reveals itself in every stage
    Of tender life and growth:
Paternal snow, maternal green
Lend twofold beauty to thy mien,
And tho' thy cast toward her lean,
    Stamp thee as born of both.

Methinks he, stern and gloomy, kept
One day's bright jubilee, and wept
Impassioned tears as thou up-leapt
    In such ethereal grace,
The while she kissed and fondled thee,
Well pleased that, tho' ill-mated, he
Ere dying, left as legacy
    His look in thy young face.

To name thee, Heaven and Earth may yield
Fair types—a sacred Truth revealed;
A pure resolve or wish concealed
    Till now in some dark breast;
A maiden early called from sleep
Due matin Rites and Vows to keep;
A holy face that bends to weep
    O'er stormy Earth's unrest.

The welcome babe that first appears,
The meek girl charming thro' her fears,
The hoary Saint bowed down with years
    Each lend an image true:
But O! the sweetest to my mind
Shall feign thee one of Angel kind,
Pitched on our tearful world to find
    Sad spirits she may woo—

A lovely Seraph—for my heart
Is won by this Celestial art;
And richly does its spell impart
    Rare virtue, strength and hope,
Thy solitary beauty, hid
From common criticism, chid

My lust for eulogy and bid
    Me crave no ampler scope.

Thy purity 'mid no support
Encouraged me thro' ill report,
And scant companionship to court
    Fair Honour's snowy meed.
And, glorious truth ! wherever one
Brave flower has thus its course begun,
A bevy struggle to the Sun
    Obedient to its lead.

Ah, blessings on thee ! thou hast taught
Me patience here : no holy thought
Has blossomed ever but has brought
    A many in its train :
No longing steals thro' earthly rift
To claim warm Heaven's fostering gift,
But a sweet virgin host uplift
    Meek prayer, nor sue in vain.

Scarce ever bitter trouble froze
A human life, but there uprose
Some budding whiteness to unclose
    In flowering beauty soon :
And never knew I one bright spot
Discerned, but swift the saddest lot
Was gemmed with springing joys begot
    By musing on that boon ;

As 'mid eve's deepening shade the eye
Scans the first silver in the sky

And lo ! a throng steal forth to vie
  With that pure herald star :
No longer linger I, lone Flower !
Lest dreaming on, this sunny hour,
Thy sole prestige, thy single power
  A rival host should mar.

ODE TO A "STRAD" VIOLIN.

CONCEIVED in Heaven, formed on Earth,
Immortal Genius gave thee birth !
Rich tone, rare fashion stamp thy worth
  And prove thy pedigree.
It may be Nature's music clings
Round even severed sylvan things,
And so perchance thy substance brings
  A boon from land and sea.

This frame, so exquisite, long stood
Mid the arboreal brotherhood.
Steeped with the warblings of a wood
  Nigh some soft southern wave,
A reminiscence of whose chimes
May wake strange harmony at times,
As echoes from pre-natal climes
  Lethean spells outbrave.

His hand, methinks, who carved it wrought
The true expression of a Thought

Divine, that whispering Angels brought,
    And bid him mould aright.
I deemed that Music's utmost spell
To elevate, and soothe and quell,
Was spent, until I heard thee tell
    Thy story of delight.

Ah! then I knew what wealth remains,
What potency for glorious gains,
What frenzies, what harmonious pains,
    Still tremble to my quest.
O meet to grace a Seraph Choir!
Thy magic flames me with desire
Now kindled by the master's fire
    That haunts his rich bequest;

And fed by what may linger still
From all that tuned thee to their will,
And made thee speak and wail or trill
    As passion pitched the key—
From each full heart in years gone by
Who, barred from human sympathy,
Seemed listening for a sweet reply
    To all it told to thee—

Desire that burns with feverish glow
And borrows hue from ebb and flow
Of billowy music as the bow
    All deftly sweeps thy strings:
Her changeful moods and finished art
Who wields it bids some dormant part
Of my true being wake, and dart
    To reach supernal things,

Things whose delight I can but taste,
For scarce I touch what I have chased
But it recedes in mocking haste
    To tantalize again.
So Love still beckons from the Skies,
So Beauty flashes rare surprise,
So Sadness robed in tender guise
    Taunts with delicious pain.

The Virtues many, Graces all,
Divinely sun their charms, and call
In promise of enchanting thrall
    So I but win their Realm :
Nay ! be it still unwon, there gleams
On my foiled spirit, as she dreams,
A Light, whose faintest glory beams
Earth's utmost bliss o'erwhelm.

Elusive Joys, that wizard Sound
Thus conjures up ! ye hover round
To vanish in a gloom profound
    That deepens as ye fail :
Musician fair, stem not this rush
Of melody, lest Silence hush
My heart's sweet tumult, and the flush
    Of its brief radiance pale !

IN EXTREMIS.

HER eyelids close—we think she sleeps;
But mortal guesses wrong her state:
'Tis that her summoned spirit keeps
    Tryst at the Royal gate.
Ere the Key opens, left alone
For all that human cheer can yield,
Till the fair King, the splendid Throne,
The Realm of Glory, are revealed.

See round her ashen lips the trace
Of joy and sadness, like the play
Of light and shade o'er the cold face
    Of a December day!
The shadow, born of mists beneath
The brightness, of the Sun above,
Ere chilly Earth's last vapour wreath
Has vanished in unclouded Love.

Now looking back the spirit spans
Life's weary course, from start to goal;
Now gazing wistfully it scans
    Heaven's fast unfolding Scroll.
O for a glance at Memory's book
To vision what its record tells!
O to be sharer in the look
That fronts a World where Glory dwells.

Ah! whence the evanescent gloom
That strays around her features wan?

Perhaps she wanders mid the bloom
    Of Beauty spent anon.
A gleeful child, she melts in tears,
A dreamy girl, dissolves in sighs,
A woman, feels the care of years,
The failure of some vanished prize.

A lover in some happy dell
Has wooed her—does she now re-shed
The drops that trickled at the knell
    Which tolled him to the dead?
Perchance she mourns her failings few,
For sins who dares to call them now
That Christ has stamped her gold as true,
And left His hall-mark on her brow,

The seal of gloom-dispelling Joy?
For lo! its impress now! what sights,
What sounds, what reveries employ
    Her heart, what rare delights?
Is it contrition changed to bliss,
The rapture of a Past forgiven?
Their beckoning smile, their nearing kiss,
Once from her fond home-circle riven?

The pilot Seraphs hovering near
To waft her scatheless—is it these?
Nay, 'tis His welcome sounding clear,
    His step who holds the Keys.
Her eyes unclose—one last bequest,
A faint fond farewell, meets our eyes,
And her pure spirit joins the Blest
Who reign with Him in Paradise.

ODE TO A BLACKBIRD.

TROLL out thy passion from yon vantage spray
The while I gaze on thee, and guess its theme,
Thou Milton among minstrels, whose rich lay
Bespeaks high vision, and unearthly dream !
With eyes uncurtained, thou art blind as he
To all but Heaven, tho' a faery world
Outstretched beneath thee spreads her myriad lures.
  Throned on this spiring tree
With head and form elate, and pinions furled,
Thou scornest all response to her gay overtures.

Some Paradise thou singest—is it lost
That this rare pathos steeps thy lofty strain ?
Did ever dawn a day when to thy cost
The pride of being led thee to disdain
A nobler destiny, or break some law
Of thy bird nature ? or dost thou bewail
A ravaged Eden, a sweet sylvan nest
  Spoiled by the felon paw
Of predatory weasel, or perchance, too frail
For vernal tempests, or too plain to schoolboy quest ?

Or maybe 'tis for us this plaintive wealth—
That we in wistful audience may hark back
To happier days of innocence and health :
Angel of sadness ! robed in tender black
To chant a requiem o'er buried joys,

I hear thee never but I dream of bowers
Dismantled and forlorn, of beauty fled,
    Of love that sin destroys,
Of gardens serpent haunted, fading flowers,
And outcast feet in funeral march toward the dead.

And yet that music! Paradise regained
Pulses thro' all; and fitly does the trill
That comforts thee, and keeps our heart enchained
With sunny hope, rise from a golden bill,
A tongue of flame, so eloquent that thou
To melancholy must have bid adieu :
Ay, Earth holds joy enough to make thee glad—
    A mate, perchance, with vow
Inviolate as thine—none, none could woo
With such delicious breath, who lingers lone and sad.

Nor could thine audience nurse a woeful Past
A gloomy Present : who can fail to feel
That Evil's haunting curse shall never last—
That strenuous Life shall break the mortal seal?
Our wintry world shall flame to Love's embrace
As Earth now flushes to the kiss of Spring !
Thou high Evangelist whose mellow tale
    Thus charms my listening Race !
No loftier pæan did rapt Milton sing
Of Grace, our sad apostacy to countervail.

So I, who first grew pensive, leave thee glad,
Thanks to thy homœopathy—that voice
Which thro' its tinctured sadness, heals the sad.
Its haunting cadence lingers, " Be thy choice,"
It pleads, " not vain regrets, but Heaven's new boon ! "

Ah! what has scared thee? flitting down to Earth
All seems the poorer for thy hushed refrain:
    Yet shall that silenced tune
Survive immortal, as befits its worth,
Resounding thro' the echoing arbours of my brain!

A PARADOX.

TILL Memory die one spot I shun;
While Memory lives it is the one
    Where brightest hours are passed:
The scene where life's best tale was told
I never would again behold;
Yet there I linger as of old—
    Shall haunt it to the last.

You ask me why and how! 'Twas there
I fathomed hope and gauged despair,
    Won wealth, knew bitter loss.
There sparkled many a vanished face;
There flourished many a withered grace;
There hovered many a joy whose chase
    Beguiled woe, care, and cross.

To see it now were but to vex
Fond eyes with vision of sad wrecks,
    Rude changes, vanished blooms:
Who seeks the ruined site where grew
Spring buds of white, and bells of blue?
The ground where summer roses blew
    None haunt 'mid wintry glooms.

Yet in whose brain-world lurks there not
The image of that garden plot
    With amplest charm bedight?
'Tis such a scene that I frequent;
'Tis there the happy hours are spent;
There live sweet blossom, song and scent,
    Fair forms and faces bright.

'Tis always summer, always wealth,
Hope, love and beauty, joy and health,
    Flood tide, bright sun, full moon:
No thunder-cloud, no stormy wind
Stain that blue heaven in the mind;
No frown, no word or look unkind
    Distract that soul commune.

Ah! strenuous Will, so prompt to bar
The passion that intrudes to mar,
    The tears that fain would flow—
Kind Memory too that in soft ways
Smoothes out all roughness from those days,
And wraps them in a tender haze,
    To ye this heaven I owe!

ODE TO SPRING.

HARK! did ye hear them—the rumours afloat
Of her near advent? Yon gossiping trees
Murmured it then—while that robin's clear note
Preached a soft gospel, retold by the breeze:

Steal on, sweet Spring !
Each wistful thing
Knows the glad secret—descend on bright wing !

Glance like a sunbeam whose life-giving ray
Slants thro' the mist to unchain fettered Earth !
Flash her to freedom, as on the set day
Prisoners are lit to new life, hope, and mirth !
Field, wood, and stream
Gild with thy gleam !
Flush them with beauty like love in a dream !

Lighten grey Earth till her slumbering face
Wears a new glory, as when some dark soul
Wakes to self-knowledge, or glows with rare grace
Born of the fire that from Heaven she has stole ;
Or lends due scope
To some faint hope,
Potent a world of delight to unope !

Greet patient Earth with a lingering kiss !
Long has she looked for thy promised return,
As a girl sighing for sisterly bliss
Peers from afar a faint form to discern.
Let each fair face
Fondly embrace,
While all stand 'mazed at such ravishing grace.

People dull Earth, as a genius his theme,
Fertile in blossom and life at his spell !
Paint her as when a true artist his dream
Seeks on bare canvas divinely to tell,

Till the world pause,
In rapt applause,
At the rare charm of the picture he draws!

Bid silent Earth with new music resound!
As a lorn minstrel, whose tuneful heart thrills
To passion glances, sheds melody round
Fraught with sweet echoes that faint in far hills.
Mate all the lone;
Each with its own
Chiming Love's pæan in manifold tone!

Hasten, bright Fairy! unfetter my heart;
Rouse it from slumber; caress it to health;
Throng it with beautiful thoughts and impart
To its fresh dreams Colour's loveliest wealth;
Quicken its dower;
Lend it new power
Bird-like to sing mid its own fragrant bower!

PRÆTERITA.

SOFT airs that fan the face
Fraught with the wealth of Space,
Lightly shed three-fold grace
O'er fevered sense—
Faint music, subtle smell,
Wafted wings, breathe a spell
Each from rare joys that dwell
In clime far hence.

So from the languid Past
Blows many a perfumed blast
Too exquisite to last,
 All too divine :
Could ye but linger, Earth
Renewed in Heavenly birth
Would smile in tearless mirth
 On hearts that pine !

Echoes as yet unspent
Of the tones softly blent,
That once to being lent
 Virtue and charm !
Whiffs of the scent that clings
Round sweet half-faded things !
How your wild magic brings
 Music and balm !

Forms in their train who come
Scarce lifeless, hardly dumb,
Calm, smiling, tearful some !
 Be your wings furled !
How can ye flit and toy,
Thrill the lone heart with joy,
Yet while with hope ye buoy,
 Turn from our world ?

Each breeze-borne butterfly
Favours both earth and sky ;
Wild shore-birds flashing by
 Settle and spread :

Alas ! must ye alone
On veering gale back flown
Leave us forlorn to moan
    O'er brightness fled ?

TRANSFIGURED.

I WATCH a ball by rampant feet
    Tossed wildly to and fro,
The mad advance, the grim retreat,
    The frenzied ebb and flow.
I hear the loud huzzas that greet
    Heroic friend or foe.

And lo ! the field becomes the World ;
    High Heaven my vantage ground ;
The ball thus bandied, carried, hurled,
    A soul mid earthly round ;
The sides against each other hurled
    With shame or honour crowned,

Embattled angels, these of Light
    And those of gloom, full strong,
This side, to near the goal of Right,
    That side, the goal of Wrong.
While clustering near to view the fight
    Are ranged a spirit throng.

God ! how they strive and strain and press
    Who the weak mortal claim,

TRANSFIGURED.

Now grasped by Evil's utmost stress—
    Heaven mar its force and aim!
Now at the feet of those who bless—
    Christ speed them to the game!

Cheer them, pure Spirits! Like the sun
    Flash out in glory blaze!
Joy! Time is over, they have won!
    Their charge they hold and raise!
While echoing plaudits, now begun,
    Shall chime eternal Praise.

THE SISTER OF MERCY.

SHE has shone, as glows Dawn's fairest blush,
    On the Night of my sorrow:
She has gone as goes Eve's rarest flush
    That scarce hints a bright morrow.
And behind her remains a bequest
    Like a June day's spent story,
The reminder of pains that she blest
    With bright Noon rays of glory.

Low tones came like Music's rare spell
    To soothe sad emotion,
No moans from light zephyr e'er fell
    More smooth on mad Ocean:
Then a rush of meet words filled my breast
    For a time with strange yearning,

Like the gush of sweet birds who to rest
  With soft chime are returning.

Pain and anguish I woo if they send her
  In light so Elysian,
Fain I'd languish anew to engender
  New sight of the vision !
Each look, if revived nevermore,
  Each tone if it perish,
In the book where is hived a sweet store
  Fond Memory will cherish.

IMPERFECTION.

EARTH vaunts no joy that lasts,
  No charm all fair ;
Light that no shadow casts
  What eye could bear ?
Sweet grace and sad decay,
Cloud pierced by golden ray,
Light and Shades' tender play
  Blend in each day.

Gladness is sunshine soft,
  Whose genial beam
Bids a wild desert oft
  With blossoms teem :
Yet colour, form, perfume
Flourish thro' mists that loom ;

Beauty's coronals bloom
  Mid transient gloom.

Goodness is Light Divine,
  Evil its shade ;
This destined more to shine,
  That more to fade :
Fleeting the chequered scene,
Final a Clime serene,
Light tempered by no screen
  For eyes full keen.

Hence ! what retards that rule ;
  Hither ! what speeds.
Mortals ! shun no dark school
  That glory breeds.
Eyes with sad dewdrops wet,
Minds scorning to forget,
Hearts pining with regret,
  Bliss waits you yet !

LOST AND FOUND.

I FOUND it yesterday, the Book
That "with a Mother's blessing" traced
Upon the title page, I took
  When first the world I faced ;
Young, thoughtless, gay, I little dreamed
With what delight the Volume teemed ;
I guessed not, till I bid adieu,
The Blessing's worth, but then I knew—

I knew it mid the loneliness
Of vanished smile and voice—I felt
That something of her last caress
   In those dear pages dwelt—
Still dwells, for when the Volume came
To light, it lingered just the same;
The magic of her prayers and tears
Had vanquished the decay of years.

I knew it better in the hour
Of strife with many a battling sin;
That Blessing chilled the flaming power
   Of fire that blazed within:
And best I knew it when I conned
The glorious words that she, with fond
Appeal, had bid me learn and store;
Whose beauty won me more and more.

She meant it as a lifelong charm—
Her Blessing blent with that high Truth—
To hold proud manhood back from harm,
   Nor only simple youth:
I might have known it better still,
But for self-seeking, and self-will:
Sad omen, fraught with fatal cost
That Book unstudied, slighted, lost!

But now 'tis found again—O Joy!
Is that a pledge that I once more
Find the lost wealth, that as a boy,
   I deemed it bliss to store?
Ah! happy he, who, alway wise
To know its value, never sighs

For what the false World reckons gain,
But which the Truth has stamped as vain.

Blind fools, we have to handle dross
Before we know the feel of gold ;
True opulence we scorn, till loss
    Its empty tale has told.
Dear Mother ! dost thou see me now ?
And canst thou hear a contrite vow ?
Mark these sad tears, this late regret,
And know thy Blessing haunts me yet !

HINC ILLÆ LACHRYMÆ.

EMBOSOMED deep it lies, the fount of tears
    Untapped for sterile years,
      Till floating down from God
One hovers o'er the arid human sod,
Equipped methinks with a divining rod
      That pointing truly, lo !
The spring is won, and soon refreshing waters flow.

They flow, the ready tears, at his behest
      From the impassioned breast,
       Flow lightly, sadly oft,
Now in full volume, now in trickling soft,
Unstemmed though angels frowned and demons scoffed,—
      To-day, in wild despair,
To-morrow, in some darling hope none else may share.

Upwelling, oft unwillingly they rise
    And brim the tell-tale eyes ;
    Glistening with rainbow gleam
If spirit radiance flash a happy beam ;
Or dim as bubbles on a turgid stream
    If gloom holds sunless sway,
In strife perchance lest deep heart secrets they betray.

Vain strife, ye traitor drops ! too hard the task :
    What Stoic wears a mask
    That never falls ?   The trace
Of stifled passion lingers in the face
Tho' eyes be tearless, and unruffled grace
    Hold empire o'er the form :
Chance looks, unguarded tones, bespeak the smothered
    storm.

They flow and ebb, unswayed by tidal laws,
    And oft from scarce a cause ;
    No feeling, thought or mood
But starts or stanches them—a gesture rude,
A tender glance, a dream of vanished good,
    And the weak wistful heart
Yields a fresh tribute to her lord's imperious art.

Ye ask his name ?   'Tis all-subduing Love
    Divining from above
    And sinking down—whose spell
Fails not, tho' hard the soil, and deep the well.
True tears ! I scorn you never, for ye tell
    Of pure reviving strife,
And fruitfulness, and all that drowns dark death in life.

E

HUSH !

To music we listen
From one whom I never may meet
Again,
That makes all eyes glisten
And thrills every spirit : her sweet
Refrain,
Like the mingling of viol and harp and lute,
Is soon
As tender and sad as the plaintive night birds' that salute
The Moon.

The cause of her magic
Is private to each who can feel
Her spells ;
Tones gay and tones tragic
Sound dirge-like, or else seem to peal
Joy bells :
To me warbles one who with Nature is quite
In tune,
Who wafts me the rapture of May, and the whispered
delight
Of June.

Some sweet notes arrest me,
Like echoes from field, lane, and vale
Unspent,
Of song that once blest me
From thrush, 'merle, and rich nightingale
All blent :

I am steeped with the glory of old, mid the dreams
    Of youth ;
And catch thro' the story fair Nature then told me faint
  gleams
    Of Truth.

   Some soft strains that reach me
Betoken a spirit refined
    And pure,
   And linger to teach me
The graces and charms that my kind
    Allure :
They gush from a heart that mid anguish and guile
    And woe
Is faithful, and brave, and contented to languish awhile
  Below.

   Some rare tones bewitch me
All fresh from a soul that can soar
    At will—
   Return to enrich me
With calm from the passionless Shore—
    And trill
To all who lend audience, some tale of that Clime
    So fair,
In music that seems a sweet snatch of the ravishing
  Chime
    Sung there.

NATURE'S INSURGENTS.

YE mighty Powers that haunt us,
In seeming aim to taunt us
With impotence, or daunt us
    If we outfly your rule !
Had Fate to being brought me
In times when seers had taught me
That gods thus fought or sought me,
    I scarce had been their fool.

I soon had learnt to sunder
Jove's wrath from gale and thunder :
Urania's gaze had wonder
    But never homage bred.
Still as in legends hoary,
Too oft ye shame our glory,
Disdain weak Virtue's story
    And lift proud Vice's head.

Skies laugh o'er war-fiends raving
And flags of victory waving :
Gloom clouds sweet Saints while saving
    The wounded, dying, lost.
Wrong journeys mid controlling
Of storms, else fiercely rolling :
The route towards heart consoling
    Is travelled tempest-tossed.

Soft lyrics from the bower,
Rare perfume from each flower,

Lend magic to the hour
 When Love's true tale is told :
Yet stainless blue is spreading,
And softest airs are shedding
Full charm on false hearts wedding
 For pomp or place or gold.

Apollo's glow is brighter
Oft, and pure Dian lighter
When Hate the disuniter
 Parts twain, than when Love links.
Cold glitter, heartless gleaming
That mock our Passion's dreaming !
We, musing, planning, scheming,
 Return your scorn, methinks.

What recks the smiling Ocean
Of their disturbed devotion,
Wrath, envy, wild emotion,
 Who range yon golden sands ?
Nor will they mind his frowning,
But risk harm, danger, drowning,
If Love relent in crowning
 Heart troth by clasping hands.

No lark that sets Earth ringing,
Or blithe finch, pause in singing
To heed the mourners bringing
 In tears their coffined freight :
No spasm of Spring weeping,
No mist o'er graveyard creeping
She minds who, vigil keeping,
 Sits lone from Dawn till late.

We sow, we reap; disdaining
Fair sunshine, or foul raining;
Our feet despise enchaining
    By fetters cold or hot:
Life's cordial tonic taste we,
Each on his mission haste we,
Nor, tho' ye baulk us, waste we
    Tears o'er our fitful lot.

False Powers, your guile defying,
No stress, alive or dying
Shall drive me to relying
    On your capricious Will!
Love! be we true together,
And mock we empty tether;
Then calm or stormy weather
    Shall find us restful still.

DISILLUSIONED.

WE slumber in youth
To the pathos of Life,
Starting up to its truth
Oft mid anguish and strife.
Man's levity reft thee
Of girlhood's fresh mirth:
A woman it left thee
To face a changed Earth.

Love shone on thy sleep
Like a dream of delight,
When faery spells steep
All in marvellous light :
Its witchery banished
Sane thought till Daybreak ;
The vision has vanished
And thou art awake !

Awake—and behind thee
The glory untold
Whose rays still half blind thee,
Whose fainting gleams fold
Thy spirit in splendour,
As warm afterglow
Wraps in hues soft and tender
The cold Alpine snow.

Ah ! cold as bleak Earth
To thee soon must appear
When Dawn's languid birth
Grows to Light strong and clear :
Fresh roused from sweet slumber
With eyes wild and wet,
Art thou of the number
Whose hearts can forget ?

Nay ; thine, if I gauge it
Aright, is too true :
Will aught disengage it
From bitter review ?
The image once traced
In firm lines will remain :

If ever effaced
It would haunt thee again.

O loath to surrender
A charm that has blessed!
Too constant, too tender,
For aught but unrest!
So flavourless all
That once made thee gay,
To a heart steeped in gall
What, what can I say?

This only—the Power
Who moulds from above
Shaped all to this hour
Of lingering love—
Thus emptied of pleasure
To garnish for Joy—
Thus robbed thee, for Treasure
Unmarred by alloy.

Firm Joy, no emotion
Of varying mood—
Wealth won by devotion
To militant Good—
Strange virtue, rare beauty
In Piety lurk;
Balm lingers round Duty,
Grace circles true work.

A Morn glows before thee
Too brilliant for dreams:

The Sun that shines o'er thee
Mocks Sleep's fitful gleams :
If music could thrill thee
Born wholly of night,
Day's Anthems shall fill thee
With speechless delight.

Full long did'st thou languish
And breathe empty sighs :
Regret not the anguish
That opened thine eyes :
Nor rue the ideal
Still sceptred within,
If Good seem more real,
More worthy to win !

And what if the passion
That flames thy lorn breast
Serve more than to fashion
The soul to be blest—
Serve more in far days
Than a point sad and sweet
For the spirit's back gaze
And the heart's fond retreat.

What if Love be a token,
A prophecy sure,
Of union unbroken
Hereafter ? nay, more,
What if true hearts once dreaming
In pureness like thine
See thro' shadows the streaming
Of Glory Divine ?

TEARS.

TEARS born of wild emotion
Rise from the storm-tossed mind
As briny spray from Ocean
　　Swept by tempestuous wind :
But lo ! as Day advances
Each spell-bound billow dances,
While Joy's fair sun out-glances
　　From angry clouds behind.

Tears, born of sullen anguish
Back waving sympathy,
Ye cling like mists that languish
　　To damp autumnal glee,
O'er earth and wave a-tether
For long sad days together !
Ah ! when will clearing weather
　　Turn gloom to jubilee ?

Tears shed in saintly sorrow,
Stemmed by absolving Grace,
Yet still undried, ye borrow
　　An emblem from Earth's face,
When she, Dark's empire scorning,
On some pure summer morning
Wears as a meet adorning
　　The dews her Sun shall chase !

Tears for heart-rapture vanished
Like dews of evening fall,

When sunlight spent has banished
  Escape from dusky thrall :
O dreary weary waiting !
O gloom with no abating,
Gloom ever instigating
  Sad Memory to recall !

Tears born of no repenting,
But empty sheer remorse,
Ye seem the unrelenting
  Of a day's hopeless course,
When fall of leaves and stripping
Of blooms chime in with dripping
From leaden skies equipping
  New vapours with new force !

Tears born of Joy's o'erflowing,
His tale too rudely told,
Seem drops that prime the glowing
  Meridian skies unfold :
From Noon's laboratory
A cloudlet veils the glory,
'Tis but a moment's story
  And all is stainless gold !

A TWILIGHT MUSING.

YE who in this vain life
Once shared my joy and strife,
  Where are ye all ?

If as the stars ye shine,
Steeped in pure light Divine,
Ever on me and mine
    May your beams fall!

When care or ills and fears
Quicken our mortal tears,
    Wake high desires!
Yon silvery watchers lend
Heaven's delight as they bend;
So may our hearts ascend,
    Lured by your fires!

When ye who view Earth's whole
Chance on a hapless soul
    Faint and astray,
Rescue from mortal harm;
Bid hope all fear disarm;
Spend your divinest charm,
    Your saintliest ray!

When vexed by rain and gale
Thro' the dark stormy veil
    Skyward we turn,
May a kind rift reveal
What lorn star-seekers feel,
That true mid woe and weal
    Heaven's sentries burn.

Yet tho' all hearts ye reach,
Angels of mercy, each
    Has a charge set:

Vanished ones ! what if ye,
Once passion-tossed as we,
The strugglers oversee
    Whom ye here met ?

What if two keen to scan,
Nigh when life's dawn began,
    Still linger near—
Nigh me, ere sunset fade,
Twin stars of evening shade,
Calmly to shine and aid,
    Lighten and cheer ?

A RAMBLER'S REVERIE.

WE wander up a golden lane
That circles to a mountain plain
    With peaks that spire aloft ;
For tempting berries in rare show
That round the fertile lowlands grow,
Fast ripening in the autumn glow,
    We linger long and oft.

Gay hearts, we hold our sunny way
While music leaves each lip, to stray
    In faery echoes round :
Bewitched by gleam and perfumed breeze
We " lotos-eaters " bask in ease ;
All thorny stress we shun, to seize
    The fruit no brambles bound.

Tho' for one mellow prize a score
Half ripe will harm us, tho' no more
    We sweep the teeming hedge—
Tho' mid the briers, as by stealth,
Profusion peeps in purple wealth,
Fraught with no injury to health,
    Of fruitful toil the pledge.

Vain triflers we, true type of those
Whose Paradise is base repose ;
    Who skirt the realm of Thought,
For ever children—tho' adult—
Disdainful of the ripe result
Of latent germ, and growth occult,
    By wise deep thinkers taught.

Ay, and true emblem we of all
Who, duped by sense's weakening thrall,
    Neglect each bracing chance—
Pluck mirth at cost of after sigh,
Hid opportunities deny,
Potential pain-wrought bliss pass by
    With half-averted glance.

To height o'er height our souls must climb,
Each teeming with new wealth that Time
    Shall open to new gaze.
Earth's plenty ripens to endow
Man for the Mount's first level b
This Life-lane is but traversed n
    For back none ever strays.

AN ANGLER'S SOLILOQUY.

BRIGHT fish, weak victim of my wiles,
How comes it that my art beguiles
　　The wariest of thy race?
Let mine return the answer: we
Are charmed as readily as he,
　　And snared to our disgrace.

Some lovely morn Life's rippling stream
Divinely glistens and we dream,
　　Nor reck that baleful eyes,
Keen to allure, have marked our state,
And deck some bright bewitching bait
　　In Beauty's fairest guise.

Lo! Passion suns his splendid wings;
Or Pleasure flaunts gay burnished things
　　With soul-enchanting look:
Life's smiling water flashes fire;
Who thinks his throbbing heart's desire
　　Masks a deceitful hook?

Who reckons with the fiendish rank
That stud our mortal being's bank,
　　Each dangling some rare treat?
God! how they dance before our eyes,
And skirmish till our spirits rise
　　To front the gaudy cheat!

"Such hues, such radiant wings unfurled,
It must have flown from a true world!"
 (Craft hears with bated breath;)
The vision meets our wildest hopes;
Our spirit upward darts, and opes
 To drink in painted Death!

Mad Evil on the shore gives play,
And chuckles as we glide away;
 Too late! yet no!—the snare
Kind Mercy counteracts perchance:
And now when sunny wavelets dance
 Our hearts of Guile beware.

LE RAPPROCHEMENT.

SWEET! I linger, but for thee
Cold and sad like yon grey Sea.
Very life sleeps in thy love,
My best merit far above,
Far as the high Sun now lending
Hope of a divine descending.

One fond look, that ere I go
I may glisten in its glow!
Storm clouds brooding all the day
Oft have quenched a struggling ray;
Yet ere Sun and Sea are parted
It one kindling glance has darted.

One soft sigh before I leave,
Like a wistful breath at eve,
That when joyless gloom has cleared,
And the Sun and Sea have neared,
Seems to ask in plaintive wonder,
How the two could sulk asunder!

One embrace before we sever
For lone hours, perchance for ever!
Night draws no sad curtain mist
Till the two aflame have kissed:
Ere I sleep, let such a greeting
Pledge us a bright morrow's meeting.

MUSA MARINA.

DANCING waves! still the moan
Constant in undertone?
Sparkle and glitter belie your complaint—
Prove that you heave no sigh
To the fair brooding Sky
In this wild music, now loud, and now faint.

Nay, let me deem you strong
To bewail mortal wrong,
Endlessly echoing Nature's distress:
Earth shall forget her pain
Ere Ocean hush his strain
Chiming in sorrow, since powerless to bless.

F

Ay, and how could ye pause
While everlasting laws
Bid you lure Beauty and Strength to their doom?
Can ye engulph the brave
And with remorse not rave,
Nor chant a requiem over their tomb?

Mourners bedeck dear earth
With Easter's flowery birth;
Ye, sweeping all, rob sad Love of fair scope;
Since ye leave naught but shore,
Till ye our dead restore,
Let Grief's wild symphony blend into Hope!

Musing too by your brink,
Kind Waves, I love to think
Ye lend a voice to my heart's silent wealth—
Shed some wild rainbow tears
For its poor doubts and fears,
Foam with delight when its ill yields to health—

Scarce have I felt a loss
But your despairing toss
Sympathy offers unshared by my race;
Scarce have I known a gain
But a mad hurricane
Sped you to greet me in riotous chase.

Apt to sink, prone to soar,
Now clear, now clouded o'er,
Restless and yet never rampant for long;

So like my spirit, vext
One day and calm the next,
Is it so strange if her tones be your song?

What if ye moan like this,
Plaintive mid seeming bliss,
Failing of peace till the Sea be no more,
That she may heave no vain
Sigh for release from pain,
Tossing this side of Eternity's shore?

HIDE AND SEEK.

NIGHT, of nights that were and are
Tenderest, best!
Bid clear moon and silvery star
Aid his quest.
Pledged to seek the trysting grot,
He is waiting, she is not:
Has her truant heart forgot
To be blest?

Soft winds! are a lover's sighs
Kindred breath?
Then, or passion-sick he lies,
Save from death:
Ere its last his bosom heaves,
Blow aside yon masking leaves,
Blabbing not, as he perceives
What he saith.

Breathing not her charming fright
　　　When her guile
Stands unveiled, nor his delight
　　　At her smile;
Guilt its penalty has brought,
Yet, kind gales, pray whisper naught
That she suffers (now she's caught)
　　　For a while!

A DREAM OF LIFE.

OUR Time-career is yon dark cloud
That the imperial sun allowed
　　　To float a little while,
And melt away—our Being true
The arching heaven of boundless blue,
　　　Whose beams for ever smile.

Yet the sad gloom whose vapours stain
The glorious azure is not vain,
　　　But fraught with boon for Earth;
To shed revival, shade from glow,
And temper light, that all below
　　　May feel its quickening worth.

Ah me! is life so full of tears,
So fraught with passion, grief, and fears?
　　　Then may the drops that rain

From these sad eyes, from this soft heart,
New vigour to the world impart,
　　True weal, and fertile gain!

So let me live that all may count
The effluence from this vital fount,
　　Refreshment and not gloom:
May no rude deluge from it stream;
No thunder roar, no lightning gleam,
　　Be harbinger of doom!

Nay, let my life drop glistening dew,
And let sweet sunbeams struggling through
　　Oft witness to the Light;
At darkest be it glorified
And golden rimmed, since all behind
　　The veil is radiance bright.

May wanderers o'er Earth's torrid waste
Beneath its shadow sit and taste
　　Cool ease and sweet repose;
Friends resting there more friendly wax;
Stern enemies their frown relax,
　　And rise no longer foes.

Yet, Source of all things! life should be
Upwafted ever, nearer Thee,
　　As yon calm cloud ascends:
And if this brooding being kissed
Earth once, too like a clinging mist,
　　So nevermore it blends;

So nevermore like a damp pall
May it press down and darken all
    That underneath it pine;
But rising as it speeds or drifts,
True to the cradling wind that lifts,
    Grow more and more Divine.

May charmèd dreamers gaze above,
And lovers learn a holier love
    From tinge, and glow, and ray:
Let strange entrancing lights and hues
Bring Heaven before the hearts that muse,
    The eyes that upward stray.

Yet they who look shall look again
Ere long, and feel the quest is vain:
    Absorbed in the Expanse
Whence it appeared, my vanished life,
Its melting free from storm and strife,
    God grant! shall mock their glance.

TO THE POSTMAN.

MOST welcome of all sights and sounds
Thy form and knock, whose daily rounds
    Cheer Life's monotony!
Thy mission genders many a thought,
And type by cunning Fancy wrought,
And emblem back to Memory brought,
    I know not how or why.

Dark Fate, whose store no mortal knows;
Full-handed Fortune, who bestows
    Her favours as she will;
Chance, fraught with utmost woe and weal;
Blind Justice, who her heart must steel;
Bright Life, Dark Death, to whom appeal
    Is vain for good or ill.

Full-handed Peace with affluent look,
Lean War that will no parley brook,
    All in their measure lend
Thee or thy freight some likeness true.
O! hailed by many, shunned by few,
Most court thee, as fond lovers woo
    A sweet returning friend!

The Sun arises, and his beams
Dispel Night's tears and misty dreams,
    Irradiating Earth:
Thou blessed herald of the Morn,
Thy boon oft dries our lids forlorn,
Our visions dark are overborne
    By some bright tale of mirth!

The Sun descends in flaming hope
That, darkness come and gone, all scope
    For sorrow will be spent:
Thus tho' an evening missive wake
Despair, some cheer may overtake
And quench her when at Morning break
    Fresh news thro' thee are sent.

Thine advent is the flowing tide
With measured speed, and swelling pride,
　　And whiff of distant things :
Thine exodus—ah ! when one sees
Tame ebbing, silent shore, spent breeze,
'Tis the sad calm, the joyless ease
　　Thy failing footstep brings.

Thou as the wanton Wind at best,
With fragrant wealth from South or West,
　　Bringest far joys to mind :
Not ever so—thro' thee at worst
Like North air and East gale accurst,
That skim snow-drifts and ice-plains first,
　　Bleak bitter cheer we find.

As from a lonely shore, eyes sweep
For one due sail the sunlit deep,
　　So countless lingerers scan,
From solitude of bliss or woe,
Mid matin rose or vesper glow,
Thy path, to hail thee friend or foe,
　　And mete thee praise or ban.

Thou magnet of expectant eyes,
Thou monarch o'er the fall and rise
　　Of thrilling, throbbing hearts !
I crown thee true, I keep thy laws,
If at my door thy quick step pause,
And from its store thy hand withdraws
　　One note ere Day departs !

ANÆSTHETICS.

I DREAMT I saw a Healer stand,
A medicine phial in his hand,
O'er one who at his stern command
    Drained it and ceased to groan.
I woke and pondered, and the truth
Flashed on me that the direst ruth
Of weary Age, and fevered Youth,
    Scarce justifies our moan.

Soul-sick and spirit-bound we lie;
Unvisited we fade and die;
The healing draught is mixed, and I
    Now marvel that men shrink:
Take it they must—the glass we drain;
Behold it in the care, the pain,
The loss, that haunt us! and we fain
    Would push aside, nor drink.

But lo! the opium God instils,
The anodyne for sharpest ills;
They steep each potion that He fills
    From His Dispensary:
The shadowing cares due solace bring;
Pain dreaded scarce unsheathes its sting;
And ah! how quickly hearts uncling
    That vowed forlorn to die.

Between the soul, and all that grieves,
A silent sea, upwashing, heaves
A wave impassable, that leaves
    Them impotent to touch.
We think that somewhat dear must stay,
Or vital being would decay :
Time strips it off, it falls away,
    Nor feel we overmuch.

Fain would we lash our hearts to woe ;
We chide the tears that will not flow,
Or stanch too soon, we think—but no !
    Due gall is in the cup :
Why deepen or prolong Grief's spell ?
He mingles the ingredients well ;
Not ours to languish or rebel,
    But meekly drink it up.

Ye hopeless ones fear not to quaff !
Mid earth-born showers Heaven's Rainbows laugh.
" Resurgam " smiles as epitaph
    O'er every buried boon.
" In rarer form, in purer guise,
Again in some dark hour I rise
To bless thee, as thro' midnight skies
    Upsteals the saintly Moon ! "

THE PROMISE CHECKED.

ALAS! for stifled Love, as tho' dull Earth
Enamoured of the Night, and dusky Ocean
In Litany of seeming self-devotion,
By some dark magic should retard the birth
Of struggling Dawn, that lends a golden worth
To Beauty dreaming on the misty plain,
And Grace in sullen slumber on the rippling Main.

So fares a World whose elements conspire
To check the advent of transfiguring Glory:
For rosy glow grey gloom, and self's one story
From human ebb and flow unlit by fire
Whose gleam reveals that Heavenward all aspire.
Blaze forth, bright Sun! disturb that baneful sleep
And gild the wavelets on each soul's unquiet deep.

And is *thy* life to be a day of June,
A course, tho' chequered, of celestial splendour,
Whose light is beautiful, whose shade is tender,
Where sparkling heart-waves chime in restful tune,
Where Morn impassioned yields to fiery Noon,
Whose radiance softens into Evening bliss?
Then let thy world within flame to Love's glowing
    kiss!

DIVINE PORTRAITURE.

AN artist painted a fair scene
To nature true, and human life ;
His aim, to picture one serene
Mid sorrow and tempestuous strife :
Rare genius blent with subtle art
The due expression to impart.

I marked the toil, I scanned the whole,
A stately form, a noble face
That mirrored a majestic soul
Whose truth is fused with love and grace,—
A Heaven-wrought master, who commands
The elements mid which he stands.

I may not watch His Art Divine
Nor haunt His awful Studio,
Who schemes and fashions me and mine
Mid this environment of woe ;
Yet must He His design fulfil
With closer pains and ampler skill.

A soul's pure visage blazing forth,
As perfected it views dark Earth,
The haunt of pain, and guilt and wrath,
Yet planned for a Diviner Birth :
This must employ His pencil, true
To amplest claim of form and hue ;

A lofty visage, as of one
That loves the good, nor scorns the bad,
Who, struggling like the warrior sun
Thro' evil mists, would make all glad :
A God's reserve this fitly tasks,
No marvel that the work He masks ;

For, saw we all, we might begin
To mourn that we were shown so much—
The wiping out, the putting in,
The glowing stroke, the subtle touch :
Oft mid the changes we might fail
To hold that grandeur could prevail.

Ah, faithless ! to mistrust the Love,
To doubt the judgment, skill, foresight,
That limns each feature from above,
And so transfigures wrong to right :
His pencil lingers o'er the saint,
Till beauty overpowers each taint.

BROKEN OFF.

IN the spring-time of youth didst thou bless me,
    Ere blossomed thy genius and fame ;
Fair was I, nor thou loath to confess me
    An heiress of pride in thy name.
The doom of the leaves first surrounding
    A tree, is to wither the first ;

My bloom almost spent, Time is sounding
    A death knell accurst.

Long trembles the leaf that is fading,
  Long clings to the source of its strength ;
A fate have I long been evading,
  The breeze that will part us at length.
Mine only the fainting, the grief,
  Thy beauty, thy joy, will remain ;
The tree—does it miss one pale leaf?
    My loss is thy gain.

A host green and radiant will throng thee,
  To drink in delight from thy wealth ;
For me so to linger would wrong thee,
  Nor lend me new vigour and health.
Elate as of yore wilt thou flourish
  In dreamy commune with the sky,
A-tremble, lest aught that can nourish
    Should fail of supply.

While I, losing hold of thy glory,
  From Heaven to dark earth shall descend,
Falling down, down and down, till my story
  Unblest by thy nurture shall end.
So spiritless now, that I shiver
  At even a zephyr's light breath ;
The night-gale is sighing—I quiver,
    I leave thee for death.

A NATURALIST'S GRIEVANCE.

FLAMES there are that sink and chill;
Some with years wax hotter still:
In my bosom blaze fierce hates,
That no lapse of time abates:
Foes I have, and would ye know them?
Sweep yon landscape while I show them.

Once a breezy down was here;
Once green meadows smiled each year;
Sylvan solitudes once rang
With the music fairies sang;
Sun-gilt groves and lovely places
Wooed the Muses and the Graces.

Mark the change! the waste and wreck,
At some sordid builders' beck;
Who, I ask not, lest they win
Grace, if they bewail the sin;
Cursed ruin! frown, and harden
This soft heart that else might pardon.

Yester morn, a perfumed maze,
Beauty's arbour, chained my gaze,
Haunted by sweet wealth of Spring,
Golden plume and damask wing:
Hedgers came, and tangle cherished
Yielded to the hook and perished.

Bygone summers robed fair trees
Shimmering to sun and breeze :
Woodmen felled them, and few guests,
Once their glory, weave new nests
Nigh yon fields, for ruthless farmers
Shoot and trap my airy charmers.

Perish all whose fell design
Offers Nature at Art's shrine ;
Clips the brier, trains the rose ;
Turns wild poetry to prose ;
Robs sweet earth to swell the ledger :
Woe to builder, woodman, hedger !

Sevenfold woe to all that spoil
Fresh young hearts by graceless toil ;
Stifle impulse, quench desire,
Till soft natural charms expire ;
Bury 'neath hard piles of learning
Sparkling wit, and keen discerning !

Builders ! mar no fertile brain,
Lest dark loss o'erbalance gain :
Mansions for new inmates cost
High, when native power is lost :
Like yon view with scarce a warning
Nature doffs her rich adorning.

Trainers ! keep the loving glance
Born of heart luxuriance ;
Cherish rapture, throb and thrill ;
Crush not quite the wayward will :
Tendrils creeping, clinging, twining,
Claim free play, nor brook confining.

Guardians! foster all with wings,
Fancies, dreams, imaginings:
Nature oft to airy flights
Marries music that delights,
Steeping all in tuneful glory
Like yon scene's unruined story.

So may Zephyr, Storm, and Shine—
All that figures Grace Divine—
Play in ministry of Health,
O'er the virgin heart's fair wealth,
Fresh as from its pure Creator,
Charming every rapt spectator!

A TRAGEDY.

O KING Darius! well I knew
    Last night what thou did'st feel
When on one doomed to death a crew
    Of fiends had set the seal:
While thou, unblest by lute and song,
Did'st mourn thy rashness and his wrong,
And thro' the dreamless hours did'st long
    The sentence to repeal.

But there resemblance ends, alas!
    No Daniel did I mourn;
A jealous lad whom a gay lass
    Had jilted, wild and lorn

G

Had shot her down with ripe intent;
A sheer black murder, that had lent
No plea why Justice should relent
   With glance of Mercy born.

An oft-told tale, but I had heard
   This tragedy played out:
The Jury weighed each act and word,
   Yet seemed convinced throughout:
The Prosecution, like a hawk,
In nearing zones of cogent thought,
Swooped down with aim that none could baulk,
   And slew each lingering doubt.

The verdict, who could question? Yet
   They dared to plead his youth:
Poor heart! I shall not soon forget
   Thy look of utter ruth:
I hoped awhile, but no—just men
Reprieved him not—and from our ken
He passed to be a denizen
   Of the dread Realm of Truth.

At dawn he suffered, and I tossed
   In hot unrest meanwhile;
That face my every vision crossed;
   " The moonlight, does it smile
On his last sleep? the risen sun,"
I mused, " would mock his course full run!
Grey morn! till the dark deed be done
   Day's waiting charms beguile."

I started suddenly—a screen
    Flew back, and I surveyed
In grim detail the ghastly Scene,
    To watch the last Act played:
I tried to veil it, but my will
Seemed impotent, my blood ran chill
With sympathetic horror, till
    I rose, and knelt, and prayed.

The sense-illusion vanishèd,
    Yet to Almighty Power
I prayed on till his soul had fled
    At the appointed hour.
I hear that ere he died, despair
Yielded to calm, and courage ràre;
Perchance a virtue from my prayer
    Won some absolving dower.

Ah! Righteous Love, why this twin lot?
    Why leave weak souls such scope?
Was Beauty born for that vile shot,
    Strength, for that shameful rope? '
Why fashioned thus, if thus to end?
Why bid them for a sweet hour blend,
Yet swift Love's fragrant trammels rend
    In utter wreck of Hope?

The fair Spring flowers I ever see
    Fade at sweet Summer's call;
But ah! these blossoms on Life's tree,
    That thus the twain should fall!

Not yielding to kind Nature's laws,
But victims to some awful Cause
That made to ruin—yet I pause,
    For can I fathom all?

"Thou could'st not," murmurs a still voice,
    " Yet hear what thou can'st know,
Forgetting not the while that choice
    Is left to all below!
Eternal Past and Future chime
In that dread crisis of dark Time;
They reap but what in bygone Clime
    Their spirit hands did sow.

" And for the rest, they might not win
    A nobler destiny,
Save through this agency of sin
    To lift their souls on high.
Who dreamed that he should grace a throne,
That night of old to lions thrown?"
I heard—and, like Darius, own
    One whom I glorify.

HURRY.

MORTALS! why this fierce haste
    Thro' the long hours,
As tho' by Furies chased
    From peaceful bowers?

Know ye that haste began,
When, 'neath the Eden Ban,
Fiery swords flashed, as man
   Angels outran ?

Is it the ancient curse
   Still lingering near ?
Hounding from bad to worse
   Hearts nerved by fear ;
Flaming each placid face ;
Shaming all quiet grace ;
Claiming to leave a trace
   Naught can efface.

Paradise lost forgot
   Never, by one—
Exiles from bliss, our lot
   Is but to run—
Hurry, for low and high ;
Worry in each sad eye ;
Flurry, the more we try
   Care to out-fly.

Ay, and the bane is this ;
   Dupes of false sin
Deem that through haste, new bliss
   Swift they shall win—
One must his kind control ;
Wealth is another's goal ;
Most would their worth enrol
   In Honour's scroll :

Each on another gains;
   One all outvies:
Meekness the heart disdains
   Set on its prize:
Who taught thee that, poor fool?
They, who in Nature's school
Graduate, see all cool
   And calm that rule.

Haste is their fatal mark
   Who sadly go—
Theirs who leave light for dark,
   Freshness for woe;
Clouds speeding wild and lone;
Birds across rough seas blown;
Leaves that fierce gales dethrone;
   Blossoms down flown.

What rose shuns ordered growth?
   What lily flees?
Due toil, not haste or sloth
   Hives sweet for bees;
Heaven is the skylark's aim,
Careless of wealth or fame;
Rapt hearts his worth proclaim,
   Echo his name.

No restless striving mars
   Yon regnant lights—
Pure Sun, soft Moon, sweet Stars,
   Smile from their heights,

Chiming " Spent hearts ! would ye
Look as serene as we ;
Course, and yet never flee ;
   Laugh with Heaven's glee ?

" Learn that your fevered strife
   Deepens sin's doom,
Thistles and thorns all rife,
   Brow sweat, death gloom !
Scan our Calm, and its cause ;
Keep your true being's laws ;
Revolving without pause,
   As Duty draws !"

Lo ! the heart's orbit found,
   Cherubs on guard
Frank man to Holy Ground,
   Thro' gates unbarred ;
Earth and the Curse abhorred,
Down sinks the flaming sword,
Paradise now restored,
   Enter its lord !

CONSCIENCE-STRICKEN.

THO' cool the hour, a fever blazed within
   The Pair that stood,
Stript of fresh innocence, beguiled by sin,
   Disclaimed of Good—

When lo ! His footfall, and each culprit flees
To lurk amid umbrageous fruitful trees,
Which, as the Voice floats down the evening breeze,
   Their forms seclude.

And we, their coward heirs, the guilt repeat,
   And learn the guile :
Happy and free, forbidden fruit we eat,
   And feeling vile,
Our naked spirits catch the herald stride
Of coming Judgment, and in terror hide
Mid leaves and fruitage, hoping to abide
   In safe exile.

All sweet for food, and pleasant to the gaze,
   Those trees of Joy
Dream on in loveliness, while mid the maze
   We feed and toy :
In rich profusion fruit around us bends ;
Soft Pleasure her luxurious story spends ;
Art, Beauty, Knowledge, each a magic lends
   Faint hearts to buoy.

In vain, in vain ! the fuller the delight
   The more they sink ;
For through the tangled arbour, His keen sight
   Has pierced, we think :
Else, why the awful clarion tones that sound
Clear above laugh and song mid Pleasure's round,
Forewarning us that none that Truth has found
   From doom may slink.

" Where art thou ? " so the restless, fevered heart
   Translates that Voice—

" Thou, whose rebellion merits penal smart,
        Canst thou rejoice ?"
Lord God ! before thy Majesty we fall,
Nor shirk the sentence, since we welcome all
Thy Grace provides, sad only that sin's thrall
        Became our Choice.

SUGGESTIONS OF ETERNITY.

FALSE Time, so fleet, so fugitive !
Why promise more than thou can'st give ?
Eternity, in Thee we live !
    And many an hour
The heart, attuned and sensitive,
    Thrills to Thy Power.

When on some morn elect and rare,
In radiant vision of mid air
A throng of graces fresh and fair,
    New risen, wait
The bright-faced sun, whose flaming hair
    Streams thro' dawn's gate;

Then faery-like dance in and rear
Strange figures foreign to our sphere,
Whose magic glow would disappear
    At Time's decree,
But that rapt hearts still view all clear
    That hails from Thee—

When thro' some consecrated days
The while incarnate Angels blaze,
Divine enchantment brooding stays :
     So pure the spell,
What heaven, what earth while it delays
     No heart can tell—

In some rare moment, free from shock
Of earthly ill, when taking stock
Of all Time's treasure, Love can mock
     Its best and soar
Sheer to Thy Portals, and unlock
     Immortal store—

In fevered parley with false lust
Which woos with wealth that can but rust,
When Conscience beckons from Time's dust
     To Joys that live,
And Truth pronounces Duty's " must "
     Imperative.

And chiefest in the hour of gloom,
Mid withered leaf and fading bloom ;
When woe for weal leaves scanty room,
     Thy glory lends
A Vision fair beyond that tomb
     Where Time's all ends.

ODE TO A THISTLE.

NAUGHT in fell or field, I trow,
Fails of human love as thou!
Churl, why rudely disallow
    Those who pause to handle?
Fretful spleen lurks in thy look;
Rightly is thy haunt forsook;
Those alone thy malice brook
    Cased in glove and sandal.

Who shall sorrow if thy fate
Be to perish soon or late,
When some beast of vile estate
    Straying near beholds thee?
Yet there lingers by thee one
To admire what others shun—
Brave to scrutinize, where none
    Pondering enfolds thee.

Still when I recall thy birth,
Evil's yield from cursed Earth,
Alien from all charm and mirth
    Man may well regard thee;
Type of Sin, with spines beset,
Wooed by none without regret
Piercing pain and eyelids wet,
    Fitly all discard thee!

Fitly, were it not for this
That thy purple bloom I wis

Figures the imperial Bliss
    Stored for Virtue reigning,
Virtue, born of primal sin,
Thorn-begirt, secure within,
Meekly stealing up to win
    Beauty by self-training—

Beauty open to a Sun
Cheering once, slow growth begun,
Smiling, now the Crown is won,
    Dower of glory lending—
Beauty, charming each who brings
Sense to prize pure simple things—
Beauty wooing golden wings
    O'er its secrets bending :

Ay,—hold not the fancy vain
If this field seem Heaven's Plain
For the hour, and yon bright train
    On the blossoms brooding
Be fair Virtue's suitors all
Basking mid her honied thrall,
Spirits risen from the Fall,
    Earthly chains eluding !

Sharper thorns beset the Rose,
Queen of every flower that blows.
Scarce a fairer field bloom grows
    Than thy summer story—
Blossom charming radiant bees ;
Down unravished by the breeze ;
Fluttering goldfinches that seize
    Many a silken glory.

Scotland! sure an instinct true
To this plant thy children drew:
For its story tells how grew
    The high Truth they cherish:
Emblem worn in cap or breast,
Well reminding how the best
In each heart and life is blest,
    May it never perish!

Yea! live on thou regal Flower,
Who hast flamed me for an hour
With imaginings to dower
    Hearts till now disdaining!
Some thy rule may cease to scorn—
Musing, that, without the thorn
Virtue could no soul adorn—
    And salute thee reigning.

NATURE'S RETICENCE.

SILENCE golden is, I say,
With strange meaning, in new way.
Dawn's bright face has more to tell
Than a wealth of words could spell;
Evening's tender glow has brought me
Lore that language never taught me.

"Coming" gaily chimes the one
Eloquent of Day begun;

Music of the wave and breeze,
Trill of warblers, plaint of trees,
Silent to me, save in sending
This one message thro' their blending.

Coming! who, what, far or near?
Ah! your song is silence here.
Tongue of Sphinx or Gorgon face
Whisper more than your calm grace.
Naught but life's unfolding history
May uncurtain that dark mystery.

"Going"—thus the other sings,
Eve with her soft fading things,
Vocal in sad quiet ways,
Fainting amber, deepening haze,
Tideless strand—*this* telling only
To the pensive and the lonely.

Yet your tranquil beauty speaks
All the ravished spirit seeks:
Foiled of what the mind would know,
She reposes in your glow—
Feels that it divinely teaches
Truth that Morn and Eve o'erreaches.

Coming—naught could tell me more
Than that Time holds yet in store
Joy, like Dawn's that knows no cloud,
Destined for an evening shroud;
Richer life, as Noon's full glory:
Death, as Night ends Sunset story.

Going—none may add to this,
That they vanish, woe and bliss,
As Day's weary ones find rest,
As spent glow fades in the west,
When there steals the dusky finger
Veiling all, tho' long it linger,

What of that, if changeless Love,
Like yon canopy above,
Shed new grace, as soft Moonlight
And sweet Starbeams, silver Night?
"Speech is silvern," mid that shining
Will Heaven tell all past divining?

SOUL BEAUTY.

GRACE incarnate, Glory's heir,
Born of One Divinely fair,
Cradled 'mid the gloom and strife
Of this dark tumultuous life;
Waxing while all else is waning,
Militant till brightly reigning.

Glow of mind and flame of heart,
Splendour to the face impart
Mocking Light and Shadows' play
Or the Evening Star's pure ray—
Bid it flash in lightning glances,
Quiver as a sunbeam dances.

Form will vanish, colour fade,
Time and grief mar Youth and Maid :
Fairer gleams the beauteous soul
As she nears life's dusky goal,
Thro' Earth's tale and Nature's story
Ripened for supernal Glory.

A THREEFOLD TRIBUTE.

TO tenderest affection
  This Music owes its birth :
Two flowers inspired reflection
  With their surrounding earth :
They bring a triune token
To tell of love unbroken,
And longings which unspoken
  Might fail of guardian worth.

The lily pure, disdaining
  Dark's amorous advance,
Shrinks up as tho' retaining
  The Sun's impassioned glance :
Let Goodness only sue thee,
And with his beauty woo thee,
So Wrong, if he pursue thee,
  Shall win no countenance !

The violet, who breezes
  Lets fondly o'er her play,
From the rude blast that freezes
  Turns a shy face away :

Be thou as one all tender
When loving sighs befriend her,
But who no rough offender
　Deigns even to survey!

A flower-bespangled garden,
　The Paradise of June,
All blossomless will harden
　'Neath March's icy moon :
Thy heart be frigid never !
Bright Summer haunt it ever,
And Love crown each endeavour
　With ripe luxuriance soon.

MAY MORNING.

ONE flashed upon her dreaming
　As died an April moon,
And promised, ere the beaming
　Of May's first lovely noon,
Such vital scenes to show her,
Above, around, below her,
As scanned, should overflow her
　Sad heart with Heaven's best boon.

" I mark the doubts that vex thee,"
　So spake the seraph tongue,
" For rival faiths perplex thee,
　Each eloquently sung.

H

Unseen before thee gliding,
Do thou obey my guiding,
Thine only the deciding,
   Away! while Dawn is young."

They sought at Morn's faint flushing
   The hoary Oxford tower,
And heard the strains up-gushing
   To hallow May's prime hour,
In music pure ascending
As tho' young spirits blending
In unity were lending
   To Heaven their freshest power.

Then down a vista glancing,
   They spied a village green,
Where merry girls were dancing
   Around a sceptred queen,
Crowned as with flowers Elysian,
Born of Youth's fairest vision,
Yet in scarce veiled derision
   Of the illusive scene.

"See imaged here both courses,"
   He cried, "the twain that tempt
With silent, subtle forces;
   Of each thy soul has dreamt—
Now, like those young hearts quiring,
To Heavenly Joy aspiring;
Now throned for eyes admiring,
   And mirth that breeds contempt."

"But hence!" and on they wandered
  To haunts of sin and shame,
Where pensive spirits pondered
  With lofty look and aim.
Fair women with bright graces,
Brave men with angel faces,
Scorned the smooth World's embraces
  Vile truants to reclaim :

Next to dull homes where Beauty
  Toils on unprized, unknown,
Heedful of naught but Duty,
  Stamped as her very own—
To shops and desks where tender
And bright charms lose their splendour
That Truth and Love may render
  Full tale when all is shown.

And then to Halls where Fashion
  Reclined in gilded state—
Sweet arbours where soft Passion
  Would fain intoxicate—
Red fields where laurelled glory
Clangs forth a martial story—
Bright courts where brows ungory
  Fame's peaceful bays await—

Sweet fields where rural pleasure
  Wooes every shifting mood—
Groves sacred to the leisure
  Of hearts that muse and brood.

And then they sought calm Ocean,
Whose song inspired the notion
Of deep true glad devotion
   To overarching Good.

" Thy choice ? " he asked.   All glistened,
   Life sparkled, Earth seemed dear ;
When softly, while she listened,
   A cadence smote her ear,
A chime whose tender pealing
O'er tranquil Ocean stealing
Seemed, to impassioned feeling,
   To sound a summons clear.

" Scorn thou, in Life's fair hey-day,
   Vain sloth and hollow glee !
Hear now on this sweet May-day
   My welcome, " Follow Me ! "
Both echo it, who slighted
All that had else delighted,
Apostles Mine, united
   In saintly Pedigree."

The Angel left her, lending
   Full audience to the call—
Her pliant spirit bending
   A captive in sure thrall—
Grace, Love and Peace surrounding,
Divine content abounding,
The hour meridian sounding,
   His Promise to recall.

ODE TO THE LATEST PRIMROSE.

LAST things are ever sad :
What musing heart grows glad
    O'er lingering grace ?
Thou, with a course nigh run,
Calm as the setting Sun !
Never wore saintly Nun
    So sweet a face.

What ! an unruffled brow,
Tho' of bright myriads thou
    Bloomest alone ;
Spent are thy lovely peers,
Sundered by fatal shears,
Or ruined mid wild tears
    And stormy moan ;

Bewailed by mine and me,
Only unwept by thee
    Stamped by Death's seal,
Yet since thou couldst not save,
Seeming resigned and brave.
Ah ! o'er a nearing grave
    How shall I feel ?

Feel, if I tarry long,
Last of a sprightly throng
    Facing nigh Death ?

When the due tears that gushed
From my man's heart are brushed,
Be all repining hushed
   All rebel breath !

Mine be it, patient flower !
Like thee, the mortal hour
   Fearless to wait—
Since to true being's spring
Death is no foreign thing,
Earth frowns on all that cling
   To vital state.

Ungenial soil and clime
They who outlive their time
   Can but expect :
Each in its season blows,
Then eyes that fondly chose
Thee and me, vernal Rose !
   Turn in neglect.

Better the hidden lot
Than by a world forgot
   Graceless to stay.
Better let lovely Earth
Shed o'er the young her worth—
Smile, as before our birth,
   Long as she may :

Mine to retire like thee
Whithersoe'er it be
   Vanished ones go ;

Haunted by Peace I hold
Sweeter than tongue has told,
Till Risen, I unfold
　　New vital show!

NOT WISELY, NOR TOO WELL.

SO thou, unmindful of the Past,
Fond heart, wert wise enough to think
A woman's constancy might last
Till Fate your destinies should link!
Vain dupe! to trust the shallow vow
Of youth and inexperience.
Insane! to dream that such as thou
Wert cast for Passion born of Sense.

All pay for folly,—thou must pay
For this unwisdom, in due shame.
Would Phœbus focus every ray
On one, of all that need his flame?
Would Luna light one pilgrim home
And leave a clouded world to grope?
What Star in yon bespangled Dome
Shines solely as one wanderer's hope?

Bright Ocean woos a world-wide shore;
Soft breezes kiss no special face;
The thrush that charms thy ear will pour
His song in mine, with equal grace;

And surely never honey-bee
Held one pure rosebud his alone,
To yield her sweets at his decree
Nor even now, but when full blown.

Yet thy delusion is not vain
If thro' the evanescent thrall
Of this rash fetter, thou shalt gain
The potency of loving all.
Then back, fond fool! for ever be
One lesson graven on thy mind—
Such love is not for such as thee ;
Thy mission is to bless thy kind.

BEFORE THE SOUL'S TRIBUNAL

THE champion of a lawless crew,
A murderer, a robber, too,
Caught, tried, and sentenced to his due,
    He lingers in his cell :
This hour he dies, yet on the eve
Of crucifixion, I receive
An audience, begging his reprieve,
    Of senators from Hell.

'Tis festal tide, and one they say
Has ever been released to-day :
Of two lorn prisoners they pray
    My grace on him may light.

The other, by their malice bound,
Confronting me, they now surround,
Each baying like a hungry hound
　　Whose quarry looms in sight.

Decision is my single task,
What evil hath he done? I ask:
Their hoarse accusings plainly mask
　　Undying bitter hate.
Pure, tender, true, he has but taught
The doom of infamy, and sought
To bring whatever can be brought
　　To Goodness, soon or late.

Ah! whether of the twain? Decide,
My spirit! say—shall it be Pride?
He is the culprit who had died
　　But for this vile appeal
Of lusts and impulses within,
Sworn prompters and supports of Sin,
That throng the Judgment-seat to win
　　His sentence's repeal.

Is Pride to live, that rebel chief,
Of grace and truth and love the thief,
Who murders hope, and slays belief,
　　And officers all guile?
Shall not Life's banquet prove a night
Of Passover from Dark to Light—
The Coronation day of Right
　　Throned all to reconcile?

Ah! bid the faultless Guide be freed,
(I call him Conscience now) whose lead
Obeyed shall satisfy all need,
    And purify at length!
Fettered, tho' never breaking laws,
Silent, yet pleading well his cause,
Each Devil's advocate he awes
    And makes their claim his strength.

Barabbas, to the Cross! thy doom
Is sealed: this heart, of Pride the womb,
Shall yield it, dying hard, a tomb,
    Nor let it rise again!
But thou, the Christ within, all hail!
Thine be the Throne! the chain, the jail,
Be theirs that bound Thee. Live, Prevail,
    And o'er my being Reign!

ODE TO A RING-DOVE.

VANISH all vernal forms before the twain
That charm me peering thro' yon greenery!
Cease all May melodies before that strain!
Tho' music flood the sylvan scenery
More rare and sweet by far, the tone of this
To me, scarce knowing why, excels the rest.
Is it that theirs of mundane rapture tells,
    But thine of heavenly Bliss?
That while they sport in pleasure thou art blest,
Blest with a joy that haunts no earthly dells?

Ay, is it that thy heart, resplendent Dove!
Is cast in finer, nobler mould than theirs,
And so they trill of Passion, thou of Love,
Their tale, ecstatic spasms, wild despairs
And swift oblivion ; thine, unchanging Truth
And calm Delight, and half celestial Hope,
Whose rainbow hues have burnished thee as tho'
    In pledge, mid earthly ruth,
That Love is heir to a Diviner scope
Than mortal chains and limits can bestow!

I dare to gauge thee by our human rule—
The voice reveals the nature, nor canst thou
All artless train it, or unconscious, school :
Truth must inspire this rich, deep, tender vow
Oft told and brooded over.   Well is He
Imaged by such as thou, who sues our heart
Whose Fruit is Love ; and fitly round the throat
    That breathes such sympathy
Rests the eternal Symbol ; the high Art
That cast it stamping thine as Love's true note.

Unseen I watch thee mid the emerald maze,
Coquette with thy soft mate, around her cooing,
Then wing a heavenward flight, as if in praise
To Him who taught thee this terrestrial wooing :
The while your Agapemone I scan,
Its form the mystic Circle, and within
Two spotless eggs, as tho' to testify
    To base degenerate man,
That Love breeds pureness (Passion only sin)
Pureness like snow that wanders from the Sky.

Lo! Passion wantons everywhere, and sings
And builds in open field and sunny place;
But Love, rare Love! speed, speed, as yon soft wings
Regain their homely shade! Woo thou our Race
With privacy of blessing! In thy train
Will follow Joy and Peace, and Virtue's equipage,
And all that when Life's summer glow is past
    Shall undecayed remain:
Our hearts are thy peculiar heritage;
Thine empire is Humanity at last!

CHANSON AU TABAC.

    EXOTIC from that West,
    Which dawned on one in quest
Of a new Realm whose glories shone on his prophetic
    mind!
    A true Columbus thou,
    So potent to endow
Our vext humanity with riches none beside can find.

    The stale old world of strife,
    And care, and weary life,
Is ours in that prime half of Day which hails from rosy
    East;
    But when in westering skies
    Due Phœbus greets our eyes
The soul's horizon seems too strait; she pants to be
    released,

Released from toil and all
Her narrow earthly thrall,
She seeks an outlet for her store, a playground for her
health :
Thou blessed Pioneer
'Tis thine to point and steer
To larger aims, a nobler state, an ampler common-
wealth !

Lo ! 'tis a glory cloud,
Round him thy fumes enshroud ;
Reposing royally, by his imperial purpose crowned.
The hemispheres of Thought
And Effort are now wrought
In such sure wedlock that no room for discontent is
found.

Thro' thee the old and new
Are linked in union true ;
Calm Memory mingles Morning pressure with Eve's
fertile scope.
Their forces interchange,
And languor yields to strange
Activity of brain, and firm resolve, and lofty hope.

Rare virtues in thee dwell
Whose charm remits to hell
Dark devils of despair, and fiends that torture nerve
and bone.
And O ! thy wizard power
In many a casual hour
To call up sweet illusions that, alas rude Fact disowns !

We scan a wintry world
Whose tempest has just hurled
The last few lingering leaves of some tossed tuneless
elm to death :
Thy wand has waved, and now
Blithe birds on budding bough
Their mossy mansions consecrate with Harmony's own
breath !

Beneath thy charm, once more,
We roam a dreamy shore
Where pleading waves and plaintive zephyrs chime
with Love's soft sighs :
Thy magic spent, forlorn
We can but muse and mourn
O'er broken plight, and vanished bliss, and grey,
despairing skies.

On wreaths of final fume
Hope wings her flight and gloom
Sails in, and slowly settling down, broods o'er the
lonely heart ;
Soon, at thy spell restored,
Return, bright Joy, as lord !
While Fancy, from a fragrant clime re-chases care and
smart !

SCIENCE.

HER. Temple crowns the common haunts,
And they who deem her word Divine
Must bend to one whose silence daunts
The crowd at Superstition's shrine.

That gushing Oracle of old
Draws tender souls that will not brook
A steep ascent, a goddess cold,
Who never smiles in human look—

That seek a Guide whose sure replies
Confirm the heart's raw fear and hope,
Remove the scare that terrifies,
And find for faery dreams full scope.

The many throng her still, alack !
As in the hoary World's fond youth ;
Nor reck that her prompt answers lack
The signature Divine of Truth.

They ask in tears, they leave with smiles,
They rest and cling—what need they more ?
And so that Prophetess beguiles
The credulous with balm of yore,

Her Fane stands mid the busy streets,
With open portals wooing all :
And O the crowd one ever meets
Equipped for the delicious thrall !

I seek the True. I scale the hill
Where Science queens it in bleak state :
The path is rough, the clime is chill—
What matter so I win her gate ?

I knock and enter—lo ! she stands,
A Seeress mute, austere and stern :
I kneel—I clasp imploring hands—
" O teach !" I plead, " for I would learn."

Unmoved, she opens out a scroll :
O joy ! 'tis writ by Truth's own pen—
'Tis luminous—its leaves unroll,
And flash deep secrets on my ken.

Mine to win all by patient quest,
That touches life beneath the sun ;
And yet—and yet—this fevered breast
Still clamours for a balm unwon,

The balm my spirit craved from birth :
Ah ! empty dream to think that shine
Thrown on the mysteries of Earth
Could satisfy till that be mine.

Who—what unveils it ? for that one
Shall have my knee, my lip, my heart :
O Science ! mid thy truth, can none
Uncurtain aught to heal this smart ?

She shakes her head—she scarce has shown
The vulgar Oracle at fault :
Where shall I go ? my heart is lone,
My spirit faints, my footsteps halt.

Back to the Fane of ages? Well,
Perchance I might climb higher still,
And yet be further from the spell
That sheds relief on mortal ill.

All Nature's cures lie near at hand:
The dockleaf tends the nettle's sting;
Supply waits ever on demand;
By the hot wayside smiles the spring.

What if *this* flow gush forth so free
Because the Fountain is Divine?
What if one high credential be
The very charm that haunts the Shrine?

What if the heart's just Author deemed
That He would wrong its fairest claim
Unless to Truth's celestial beam
It glowed, and kindled into flame?

Weak Superstition! call her so;
Naught boots a name—yet what if Wealth
Through this time-honoured channel flow
From the Eternal Home of Health;—

A channel clogged, befouled, defiled,
Which naught can purge, none wholly clear,
Yet holding all that has beguiled
Sad restless souls through Time's career?

Dark Superstition! true—but Stars
Smile through the deep of midnight gloom;
And Luna glimmers thro' the bars
Of each imprisoned sleeper's room.

I

The dark expanse enshrines the Light,
That inextinguishable gleam
Which silvers o'er this dusky night
And glorifies our mortal dream.

RESTORATIVES.

WHISPER with bated breath,
As in a room of Death,
    For Joy is dead!
Roused from Love's broken trance,
Vex her with no rude glance;
Let gentle Time and Chance
    Soft balsam shed!

Hers be the freshening shower
That steeps the fallen flower,
    Bidding it rise.
Hers be the herald gleam
Of rays ere long to stream
O'er a sad wintry dream
    Of sunless skies.

Hers be the healing boon
Mantling a ruin soon
    In robe of green;
Letting no scar or breach
Frown out of Beauty's reach;
Blending the ill of each
    With the fair scene.

Hers be the best of arts,
That rejoins riven parts,
 Leaving twain one—
Nature's kind skill that mends
Whate'er rude Fortune rends :
Many a tale thus ends,
 Sadly begun.

Hers (crowning balm) be Love
Bright as yon Dome above,
 Pure, calm, and true ;
Then, for low whisper, Mirth,
Meet, not for Death but Birth ;
If Love regild her Earth
 Joy lives anew.

TO THE SKY.

'TIS Beauty's Feast to scan thy shifting play
 Of shapes ethereal, and tender tints,
And harmonies at Dawn and close of Day,
 And studies in bright colour, and faint hints
Of curtained glory destined to diffuse
Its glow o'er stormy earth in soft prismatic hues !

Source of true inspiration and false dreams !
 Bank that dishonourest never Fancy's cheques !
Fount of rare music whose perennial streams
 Enravish all that nether discords vex !

Strange Panorama of weird forms and sights
That Superstition darkly voted gods or sprites!

I marvel not that in the World's raw youth
　　Men did thee homage—some perchance from Awe,
As votaries within the shrine of Truth,
　　Or subjects haply of a Throne whence Law.
Backed by the Panoply Divine, had birth
From their capricious will who ruled a hapless Earth.

And some, tho' but a few, might rise in Love
　　To the high Spring of mortal sustenance—
When Bounty streamed might turn meek eyes above—
　　When Beauty shed her best, uplift a glance
Of thankful rapture to the home of Grace,
And find a gaze parental in thy brooding face.

And some, the many, vexed by craven fears,
　　Propitiated oft thy changeful mood,
Or saw in stormy forms the passion tears
　　Of those who strove in high celestial feuds,
In tempest heard their groans, in thunder-crash
Their shout, and caught their fiery glance in lightning-
　　　　flash.

But this I marvel at, that in ripe age
　　Man scorns thee—now that he begins to don
The virile toga, and his splendid heritage
　　Of Truth and Virtue has been entered on—
Now when he grasps thy mission, knows thine aim
That he neglects thee stands to his true loss and shame.

For slighting thee, he shuns a Healer's ways;
　　No dawn, noon, night, but thou in winning mode

Hast wooed nor won our eye, like His kind gaze
  Bent ever on poor burdened ones, whose load
Were lightened thus, but who neglect the bliss,
Or cavil when they look—I marvel much at this!

At this—that while Earth's myriads love their soil,
  The beasts that browse and muse with face downcast,
Proud Man, a Sky-born spirit, seeks his toil
  And food so heedless of the ravishment
Above around him—hurrying to and fro
Unnurtured by thy light and shade, and ebb and flow—

That he, aflame for Beauty, teazes Art
  For what thy bounty proffers without price—
That wandering through gallery, hall, mart,
  He seeks fresh combination, new device—
Spends on weak imitation, time, cost, thought,
With thee the high Original unprized, unsought—

That he, athirst for Knowledge, seeks in books,
  Vent of our ignorance, what thou wilt tell
To each meek student of thy lofty looks—
  The secrets that in mortal nature dwell;
Thy magic charming from the spirits' deep
True shades, fair images, that perish else in sleep—

That wrought for Love Divine, he spares scant room
  In his capacious heart for love of thee—
Thee that, when human love forgets to bloom
  The gray horizon of our spirit's sea
With matin flush or peaceful vesper flame,
Dost plead in glow or smile perennial thy soft claim—

Thy claim to soothe, and cheer, and lift, and ply
   Love's art and ministry—that slaves of Time,
Winged by thy blandishments, we may outfly
   This carnal chain, and win our Native Clime
And seek our Sire, and—if we must descend,
Walk Earth suffused with Light, Eternal Grace shall
    lend.

Ah! 'tis as tho' men passed a sparkling fount
   For muddy streams—as if the Orbs, that shine
To lighten all, were shunned by fools that count
   Dim lamps to yield a radiance more Divine—
'Tis like the loss of Heaven for fleeting Earth,
The choice of mortal being for the higher Birth.

Prevent it every Force that bids supply
   Wait on demand!　Prevent it all within
That hails from Him Who counts His Throne the Sky!
   Forbid it Thou! nor charge us with the sin
That what Thy Truth deems false, we reckon bliss,
And what Thy Wisdom holds our need we blindly miss!

ADORATION.

COME not too near! yon glory circled Star
   Too closely scanned might prove but common earth:
Safer to gleam divinely from afar
   Than risk the glamour of a heavenly birth:
     Come not too near!

Keep not too far! the lustre of yon Sphere
  Is faint till twilight; 'tis so far away:
Perchance 'twould glisten earlier, if near.
    Shine not at eve alone, but all my day!
        Keep not too far!

Stay as thou art! Love's telescope shall clear
  Thine aureole enough to gauge the worth
Of thy humanity: yet would I peer
    Not as one keen to measure fault or dearth.
        Stay as thou art!

Let me revere! lest frightened Love depart:
  Better my heaven her pearly ports should bar
Than aught be visioned by this wistful heart
    That seems her pure serenity to mar.
        Let me revere!

ODE TO A PAIR OF SANDPIPERS.

NO studious haunt this mossy nook!
Thought strays so from my open book
The while a calm meandering brook
        Tells its sweet story,
In soft reminder that a page
Of Nature's Volume would engage
My heart with its bright equipage
        Of summer glory.

Save for that murmur, azure sky,
And flowery bank, and radiant fly,
And gleaming halcyon flashing by
    Were lost to vision—
And what has charmed me even more,
Unconscious Beauty sporting o'er
Yon margin, migrant from some shore
    Of stream Elysian.

Long have I watched you, fairy things,
Dance down the bank with airy springs,
Then sudden arch your wary wings
    In shrilly rapture—
On stiffened pinions lightly glide,
And pitch upon the other side,
A bridegroom bent on a fair bride
    He scarce can capture!

Bring ye no lore from a far strand
That human heart can understand?
Perchance these sylphs that never stand
    In vain reposing,
These forms all tremulous, would tell
How fragile is the fairest spell—
For Beauty smiles, no sentinel
    In constant posing.

She mocks at rule, coquettes with Chance!
And vibrates even as we glance;
We look away, and lo! her dance
    Of glee is over.
And haply too that wooer's chase
Of his delight from place to place

Warns all who covet Love's embrace,
    Of Joy the rover.

Full often Earth's supremest bliss,
The hot pursuer's crowning kiss
When just within our grasp, we miss
    In empty straining.
And more—methinks this counsel ripe
Hangs on your course, gay summer snipe!
Your restless movement, slender pipe,
    And brief remaining,

Appear to bid us, guests of Time,
All buoyant from a foreign clime,
Trip innocently o'er the slime
    Around Life's river—
Now sunny side, and shady now,
Our joys whatever Love allow,
Our course one consecrated vow
    To the All-giver.

Mine be it lovely birds, like you,
To rate yon gold and green and blue
    At its fair measure—
Mine, oft mid Summer's dreamy thrall,
The shadowing Journey to recall,
Then vanish swift at Autumn fall
    For brighter Pleasure!

THE SOMNAMBULIST.

CELESTIALS must have piloted
Yon sleeper risen from her bed ;
So true and safe the way she keeps
One scarce can fancy that she sleeps :

Yet treads she with unopened eyes
The labyrinth of Paradise,
Whose Chimes but muffled music yield
To ears untuned, and almost sealed :

Her tones are not the speech of one
Illumed by an unshadowed Sun :
Her robe, for all its stainless white,
Is but the deshabille of Night :

Still Radiance falls on her, methinks,
Like sunny beams thro' prison chinks,
That chariot bright wings which glide
And dance in from a world outside :

The fitful splendour that so streams
Upon her, mingles with her dreams :
Rare visions they, that mortal art
Could never image or impart ;

Half, webs of Beauty wove within,
That chastened Fancy loves to spin ;

Half, what can dwell in human bounds
Of Treasure that her soul surrounds.

But ah ! the best to sound and view
Is but a phantom of the True—
A dreamer's wild enchanted maze—
Gleams faintly flashed thro' circling haze.

Yet must she move in Glory, while
Her lips are wreathed in such a smile :
The glitter of that robe of snow
Is all unborrowed from below.

Perchance she stole it mid high talk
With Seraphs hovering round her walk,
Who, could they err, might well mistake
Her for a sister ere she wake ;

Ay, wake ! but yet not over soon ;
Earth could ill forfeit such a boon.
For lo ! her course is common Life,
Its steps, doubt, danger, care, and strife :

The bed she rose from is the dust,
Whence spring all mortals, vile or just,
And whither they return at last,
This restless vain illusion past.

Then, wide awake shall she behold
And hear the Truth now dimly told ;
And free from all that Sense entailed
Find Heaven's Rapture Earth unveiled.

MEMORY.

THERE are who deem that Virtue's prize
In some supernal Region lies,
   Some fair unshadowed Shore—
That Vice's votaries will fall
From deep to deep in gloomy thrall:
Maybe—yet each heart holds its all
   Of bliss or woe in store.

The bliss—thy spirit hives for thee,
Who wins it, as a flitting bee
   Sips nectar from each flower.
The woe—Ah! Equity Divine
No strange allotment will assign,
But mete thee what thou madest thine
   By deed of every hour.

Stern Memory! that awful wealth,
Impregnable to force or stealth,
   Thou guardest to the last—
Thou, of close, trusty warders chief;
The robber Death, and Time the thief,
Show out the truth in strong relief
   That makes thy hold so fast.

Sad Sea! where moody waters keep
·Inviolate the spoil whose·heap

Grows mid life's calm and storms—
Seen now but as a peering eye
Lost wealth thro' limpid deeps may spy,
Or dreamily watch floating by
    Wild wreckage and pale forms.

Bleak Garden! where, mid wintry dearth,
Now germinate in fostering earth
    A million various germs;
With virtue some, for blossoms bright,
Whereon Heaven's fairest may alight;
Some, charged with poison, doomed to blight,
    Or nourish loathsome worms.

True Register! where shrouded rest
The records, secret or confessed,
    Of this terrestrial Tale:
The whole, unalterably sealed;
Some, till the mortal hour concealed;
Some, ever and anon revealed
    By half uncurtained veil.

These image thee, mysterious Force!
And stamp thee, Retribution's source,
    When Death accords thee play:
The Sea shall yield her treasured dead;
The Garden be with blooms o'erspread;
The Register uncloaked be read
    As in meridian Day.

What boot transfigured guise and state
If thine equipment ne'er abate
  Its torture or delight?
Environment, all fit perchance,
Could sharpen only or enhance;
Tartarean wail, Elysian dance,
  Spring from thy Wrong or Right.

Eternal unrelenting Power!
Thy solemn freight, thine awful dower
  Rests on the world around:
For is it but a fancy vain
That all Creation bears thy chain?
Such sadness backs the creature strain
  And steeps the common sound!

Some dim dark festering sense of loss
Its shadow ever casts across
  The glee of all that joys—
Lends pathos to their patient eyes
That minister to man's supplies—
Weighs down the lark from the blue skies—
  The throstle's rapture cloys.

Has forfeit of some higher sphere
Begot all mournfulness, each tear,
  Each silent yearning look?
I know not if the downcast face
Of meek sad flowers be fraught with grace
To bid man pause ere he retrace
  One upward step he took.

Ah me ! what dream of bitterer woe
Than bright Above to dark Below
  In tantalizing sweep?
Ye who have known a "Might have been,"
Wild eyes back turned upon a scene
Whose glory no illusions screen,
    What can ye do but weep ?

HUSKS.

    THEY will not stay,
Yon withered shells that case the ripened fruit,
To mar Earth's beauty, now their work is past—
Protectors missioned by the parent root
No longer needed. Wild autumnal blast,
    Blow all away !

    They may not cling
Too long round fast-maturing Faith, the forms
That cradle her, now shrivelled to the death :
What guardian pod outstays the stripping storms ?
Strong gale of cleansing Time, at every breath
    Bid some take wing !

    They should not haunt
Our waxing hearts, the acts of long ago :
Ills, pains, mistakes, each served its fostering end ;

The scenes are played out, let the drama go!
Hence, kind Oblivion, bid thy whirlwind send
  Each spectre gaunt!

  They must not vex
Our spiring souls, the empty dream or hope
That gilt the Past; for each enshrined a germ
Fast fructifying mid Diviner scope.
Stern Fate, whose blow ends all at its due term,
  Strew these vain wrecks!

  They cannot cleave
For long to Life's fair tree, these frames of ours;
Spent as the spirit ripens, they decay:
Yet Death, and all the desolating Powers,
Sweep on! ye can but chase the husks to clay,
  The Fruits ye leave!

A PATRIOT'S APOSTROPHE.

I LOVE thee, England, as I love
Whatever He Who schemes Above
  Has with myself entwined—
My parents, relatives, heart-friends,
Home, household—all that Nature lends,
Or Art, to charm me, or that blends
  With tone or turn of mind.

Thy beauties rural, urban too,
Have power, will ever have, to woo,
   That foreign glories lack.
Fair fragrant Clime where I was born !
To slight thee were myself to scorn ;
To leave thee is to linger lorn,
   Or speed unsated back.

My habits, methods, manner, mien,
Will be, as they have ever been,
   All English to the core ;
And so a lover, while I live,
Of thee and thine, dear Land, forgive
My truth, if, oversensitive,
   This heart a plaint outpour !

My native Realm ! I feel like one
Whose debt is silence, a true son
   Whose Parent claims his awe ;
Yet who, upon occasion, dares
To question the concerns he shares,
More bold that she serenely bears
   His blame for fault or flaw.

Thine outward guise enchains my sight,
As a fair woman's charms delight
   Home eyes that scan her form :
Art, culture, use, trim natural grace,
And score full many a lovely place,
As Character may line a face
   From spirit moil and storm,

K

Yet scarce disfigure Beauty's whole :
But ah ! that tumult of the soul
　　Has marred thy face and frame—
The surging of the many hearts,
Whose thoughts and feelings, aims and arts,
In various unity, imparts
　　A Nation's state and name.

Too tell-tale thou of bliss and health,
Foregone for pleasure, ease, and wealth—
　　Of Good at Evil's shrine.
Ah ! many a face I know has told
Of worship like that cult of old—
All, prostrate round a calf of gold :
　　Shall such a look be thine ?

But lo ! thy bearing towards the World—
Methinks that England's Flag unfurled
　　Should mean the reign of Right ;
That thou, the Christian Creed confessed,
Its obligations should attest
By true kind dealing, careful lest
　　The " Royal Law " thou slight.

Two types confront me—one, whose aim
Is but self-seeking, whose sole claim
　　To rule is wealth and force :
The other, quick to own their worth,
Yet strives that Power should give birth
To freedom, purity, and mirth,
　　In all around his course.

The one shuns toil of grace and trust,
Gives only when and where he must,
   Flames up and quarrels swift :
The other, ah! the neighbours round
Will tell, while they his praises sound
That he, where want and woe abound,
   Is near to help and lift—

That would-be foes have paused, and seen
His majesty of look and mien,
   And learnt a nobler way—
A steward wise, a faithful guide,
He sheds high influence and wide,
And larger views, that shall abide
   When he has passed away.

Behold the types! the latter thou,
I hope, as lingering on thy brow
   I mark the Christian smile,
The Institutions which proclaim
That freely, under this high Name,
Sin, suffering, ignorance and shame,
   May here their woe beguile.

I hope it, as I scan the Past,
And joy o'er Slavery outcast,
   And Woman's claim allowed,
The homage to true Honour paid,
The noble strenuous efforts made
For fair adjustment and free Trade,
   That mere self-interest crossed.

'Tis no mean triumph to combine
Self-love with Duty, and assign
   To each unquestioned scope.
For man a higher life exists,
Which by self-sacrifice subsists;
But in rank, power, and gain consists
   A Nation's vital hope :

Yet being were a worthless state,
Save that she lives to lend some weight
   To principles Divine :
Thy vision here is clear and true,
And thou, what one brave Race can do
To hold the Moral Law in view,
   Art doing, Country mine !

Art doing, in majestic strife,
To still preserve a glorious life—
   Whilst using modes and ways,
Yet under protest, which each land
Must use till all in Love shall band,
'Tis thine to teach it by the hand
   Outstretched to help and raise.

One night, before my dreaming eye,
A pale Procession flitted by ;
   And to my soul was borne
The fancy that each spectral shade
Stood for some Nation who had made
The World of ancient time afraid—
   Of everything now shorn,

Save that upon it was impressed
The special feature that had blest
   Mankind, since it had died.
Calm Beauty o'er soft Greece was spread,
O'er Rome, stern Truth, of Order bred,
While Holiness, round Israel shed,
   Seemed born of chastened Pride.

Dear England ! one fond wish for thee,
Residuary legatee
   Of all they left, but Shame—
May beauteous, true, and holy Dower
Grace a far longer lease of Power,
And then, outliving thy due hour,
   Immortalize thy fame !

Ties national may loose their thrall,
And linked Humanity recall
   Them as a youthful school :
But may it own one lasting debt,
And never, never quite forget
That all it values most first met
   Beneath bright English Rule !

CHISWICK PRESS:—C. WHITTINGHAM AND CO., TOOKS COURT, CHANCERY LANE.

SONNETS AND REVERIES.

By the same Author.

Price 5s.

Extracts from Reviews of the First and the Enlarged Editions.

Saturday Review.—"A newer claimant to poetic honours is Mr. Marcus Rickards, whose 'Sonnets and Reveries' is obviously a first volume, and one not without promise."

The Academy.—"Its first merit consists in its thoughtfulness, and in the fact that it obliges the reader to think Mr. Rickards' subjects are found among those natural objects which gave Wordsworth his best inspiration. The glow-worm suggests to him reflections that are well worth the half-dozen pages he devotes to them. There are other poems in the volume which also point to the place of woman in human affairs. The following sonnet with its apt but curious comparison of woman to a wheel, and man to an axle, is one of them—'United or Apart.' The lines italicized are singularly forcible. The first of the two italicized passages shows how capable of exalted treatment is a somewhat commonplace image; the second pithily expresses the difference between the discipline necessary for a man and that suited to a woman. Mr. Rickards is at his best in descriptions of purely natural objects. . . . No one who reads this book can doubt that Mr. Rickards has the making of a poet in him."

Literary World.—"Many of the verses it contains are of a religious and devotional nature, and some of them are very happily written."

Manchester Examiner.—"This is a volume decidedly above the average of minor verse. So much is produced now-a-days that is quite unexceptional in form, but quite without originality, that it is a pleasant change to have to say of a book that it contains fresh and beautiful thoughts."

Liverpool Mercury.—"The author is to be congratulated on the power of turning his thoughts into verses which many will read with pleasure. Somehow it reminds us of Cowper."

Liverpool Post.—"'Sonnets and Reveries' are, as a rule, stately but touching, thoughtful but tuneful, serious yet melodious. They exhibit much of poetic fire and power, subdued and modified by a graceful play of feeling, with a command of expression which charms."

Public Opinion.—"The style is good. It evinces taste in the writer."

Weekly Register.—"Here is a really good sonnet with that sweet surprise among locust swarms of current sonnets, an original idea—'Petrifaction.'"

Birmingham Gazette.—"Very considerable praise may be justly accorded to these poems. Mr. Rickards always writes like a scholar, and his power of versification is uncommon."

J. BAKER AND SON, CLIFTON.

CREATION'S HOPE.

By the same Author.

Price 2*s*. 6*d*.

Extracts from Reviews.

Spectator.—"There are fine passages in the poem, and the argument on both sides is conducted with considerable ability."

Scotsman.—"In 'Creation's Hope' Mr. Marcus Rickards has produced a poem which easily redeems the promise of his earlier volume of 'Sonnets and Reveries.' Mr. Rickards' verses have nothing in them that is conventional, except the rhymes and measures. The thought is simple, the feeling pure, the expression clear of cant."

Graphic.—"The sceptical line of reasoning is very capably followed. The poet faces a despondent pantheism with an eloquent expression of faith. Mr. Rickards' work is informed by deep and profound meditation on the mysteries of the Universe, and only a man of high culture could weave so gracefully the meshes of his cogent and subtle reasonings."

Literary World.—"A much more ambitious effort. Mr. Rickards moves easily in verse, and occasionally relieves his theme by fragments of graceful fancy."

Public Opinion.—"A fine conception, and the execution is worthy of the theme. Mr. Rickards has, in not a few instances, given us passages of much beauty and power, more particularly in dealing with Nature, and human sympathy with her many moods."

Dundee Advertiser.—"The poem indicates that the writer is a man of scholarly attainments and a truly poetic heart. Many of the thoughts and fancies are exceedingly beautiful, and always clothed in graceful language."

Devon and Exeter Gazette.—"The theme is skilfully and felicitously worked out, and while the language breathes a solemn reverence for all that is beautiful in Nature and sublime in Divinity, in places it reaches the dramatic, so intensely stirring is its quality. . . . A poem full of sterling merit."

Gloucester Journal.—"The poem reveals just the same properties which place the author's earlier poems on such a high level of excellence. Personally, we prefer the Sonnets : but that does not debar us from recognizing in Mr. Rickards' work the genius which it undoubtedly contains."

Glasgow Herald.—"The story is finely told."

Hampshire Independent.—"The poem throughout exhibits deep thought, and a masterly grasp of the truths of Scripture."

Yorkshire Herald.—"Thoughtful, scholarly, and devout."

J. BAKER AND SON, CLIFTON.

SONGS OF UNIVERSAL LIFE.

By the same Author.

Price 5*s.*

Extracts from Reviews.

Saturday Review.—" Mr. Marcus Rickards, author of ' Sonnets and Reveries ' and ' Creation's Hope,' has still further added to his literary fame. These new poems may well be said to redeem the promise of his earlier work. His verses have the merit of being the outcome of a genuine freshness of thought and feeling, and are not written solely for the sake of verse-making. The descriptive poems, notably ' Nature's Cycle ' and ' Arno's Vale Cemetery, near Bristol,' show a keen love for and observation of Nature, and considerable grace and charm of expression. They fall short of the highest descriptive poetry only from an absence of human interest and personal individuality. The ' Ode to Love,' one of the longest poems in the book, is the outcome of a singularly thoughtful and refined mind, steeped with a sense of the spiritual background underlying most earthly things."

Times.—" ' Songs of Universal Life ' strikes some notes of genuine poetical inspiration. Mr. Rickards writes skilfully and gracefully. He has a keen sympathy with Nature and with country life, and a sincere love of birds and their ways."

Daily Telegraph.—" A pleasant volume of verse, full of the same inspiration which fired Wordsworth's fancy, is published by Mr. Marcus Rickards. In the quieter walks of poetry, and especially on such subjects as come of the contemplation of Nature, he writes smooth, easy verse of good workmanship and original conception. Mr. Rickards, for instance, scores off his brother poets when he points out in some graceful lines that the sybaritical nightingale, which only sings in the most luxurious circumstances, has been the subject of innumerable odes, while the sedge-warbler has been utterly neglected."

Dundee Advertiser.—" Perhaps there is no one who is more likely to take a high place among the poets of the future than Mr. Marcus Rickards, who has just added to his former achievements these ' Songs of Universal Life.' Through all there runs a healthiness of sentiment and a human sympathy. The workmanship is excellent."

Author.—" Verses written by one who is a true lover of Nature, and who would make of the common objects which he sees around him a ladder to the higher philosophy. The poetry is simple and unstrained ; the thoughts rise at times to an unexpected level."

Graphic.—" Mr. Marcus Rickards, the author of ' Creation's Hope,' a work which we had occasion to praise cordially some time ago, gives us a volume of ' Songs of Universal Life.' He is both naturalist and poet in one, a fact which will especially strike the reader in that charming poem ' Nature's Cycle,' a delightful series of woodland pictures."

J. BAKER AND SON CLIFTON.

L

LYRICAL STUDIES.

By the same Author.

Price 4s. net.

Westminster Review.—"Mr. Marcus Rickards' latest volume of verse contains many graceful descriptive touches, and, as usual, some pleasing studies of birds, their habits, and their song. His poems are the expression of a sensitive reflective mind of much delicacy. Mr. Rickards has published several other volumes, which have been well received, for he possesses considerable facility and refinement."

Literary World.—"We find in him an ardent lover and a close observer of Nature ; on the whole, we think seen at his best in the simply descriptive passages, in which nearly all his poems are rich."

Publishers' Circular.—"The author adds to his literary fame by the production of this volume. Every student of Nature is a poet, although few are able to clothe their poetic thoughts in language so calculated to please as is Mr. Rickards'. His 'Ode to a Whitethroat,' for instance, is very pleasing to the mind wearied with the productions of most of our latter-day would-be poets, whose proclivities to Ibsenism are becoming quite nauseating."

Daily Telegraph.—"A pleasant medley of songs. The passages of rural description are the best things in the book, and in these the author shows a graceful turn of expression and a keen eye for the beautiful."

Scotsman.—"They naturally suggest Wordsworth as a basis of comparison. . . . These poems are not less instinct with the simple joys and thoughts which come to men who look on Nature with a quiet eye. Their constant sympathy with Nature keeps their interest always fresh."

Dundee Advertiser.—"Mr. Rickards is an accomplished naturalist as well as poet ; he views the humbler creation with a philosophic eye, and in their ways he constantly finds material for reflection upon the higher human life. His verses are fresh and original. There is much in these 'Lyrical Studies' that is alike worthy of the author's reputation and precious to every lover of poetry."

Western Mail.—"Mr. Rickards, like Wordsworth, goes to Nature for inspiration, and his verse his graceful and happy, refined and original, and instinct with true poetry. 'Lyrical Studies' adds to Mr. Rickards' literary fame."

Queen.—"His facility for writing verse in a smooth and musical strain is almost exceptional."

Birmingham Gazette.—"In each of Mr. Rickards' books there is plenty to study and enjoy."

Bristol Times and Mirror.—"The same refinement of language, the same delicacy of feeling, and the same chastened sentiment mark this new volume. At times the more serious flights of his muse compel us to reverent attention."

J. BAKER AND SON, CLIFTON.

www.ingramcontent.com/pod-product-compliance
Lightning Source LLC
Chambersburg PA
CBHW021135020726
47500CB00003B/1083